The Feedback Loop

Book One

Harmon Cooper

Edited by George C. Hopkins

Day 545

I'm afraid to die even though I know I can't die. This fear is what drives me to kill indiscriminately, to maim as many as I can in The Loop. The day resets at midnight, regardless of whether or not Cinderella has been laid. The difference between Cinderella's story and mine is that there are no happy endings here. There is no Prince Charming, no magic pumpkin coach to spirit me away, no light at the end of the tunnel.

There is only me, and I am royally shafted.

"Who told you my name!?" I scream into the face of the same button man I choked yesterday (and the day before that, and the day before that). "Who sent you here!?"

"Let ... Me ... Go!"

Morning Assassin spits digital blood into my face, baring his pearly whites. He is a gangly man, sharp-faced and always sneering like he's in on some private joke and I'm the sucker. I slam him against the floor once more for good measure.

Keeping one hand on his neck, I stick my finger in the air to activate my inventory list. I retrieve a pair of brass knuckles, item 229, from my list. They appear instantly on my knuckles, gleaming and ready to deliver punishment.

"I'm sick of playing this game. Tell me who sent you!"

Morning Assassin laughs as my fist connects with the bridge of his nose. His data indicates that he is an NPC, a non-player character just like all the others, a feat of artificial, game-based intelligence. *He's not real.*

A second kiss with my brass knuckles makes him laugh even harder, his teeth scatter like Chiclets with my third shot.

5

"Who sent you!?" I scream to no avail.

"Goodbye, Quantum."

Morning Assassin's bloodied lips open wide and the barrel of a gat pops out of his mouth.

He drills me in the face before I can roll away.

Day 546

I respawn a day later, the sound of feedback rippling inside my skull. *Damn the feedback.* No alarm clock wakes me; I'm up naturally at this godforsaken time, glaring at the digital sun filling my hotel room with strips of bitter light.

One must sleep, even in a virtual entertainment dreamworld like The Loop. I suppose "wait to respawn' would be a better explanation for what I've just experienced, but I like to think of it as sleep anyway. It's a nice way to remind myself that I'm human, that my body still exists in the real world.

Morning Assassin will be here soon. He comes every day at 8:05 – I expect nothing less from him today. There has never been a weapon in his mouth before, but he has killed me on several occasions.

I access my inventory list and select an ice pick – item 538 – that I found about a week ago.

My list is the only way to keep track of how long I've been stuck in The Loop. Thus far, there are 544 items in my list. I add a single cigarette from the deck of Luckies sitting on the nightstand to tally for yesterday's unexpected and sudden death. Now there are 545 items. I'll find something later today to mark day 546.

It's the only way to keep track of how long I've been imprisoned.

8.05 AM. Morning Assassin smashes through the window, just as he has done the last 545 days in a row. I'm behind him in a heartbeat, driving the ice pick into his NPC skull He jerks once, twitches and falls; I'm unable for the 546th time to get information out of him. I can try again tomorrow morning.

7

My Loop-life is planned to a T. Once I kill the assassin, a crow flies by the window over my bed. It lands on the ledge outside the window, pecks its filthy beak against the glass. A dark cloud passes in front of the sun, ready to add downcast rain to the shit-stained streets outside the hotel. From there it's to the dresser.

Dressing in the Loop is a snap; it's automatic. In the blink of an eye, I'm in a pair of black boots with loosened laces, stompers with steel toes. My mirror tells me that my hair is already slicked back, my skin almost translucent, my eyes dark, lifeless, dull, sorrowful, frosted. I can change any number of the things through my attributes menu, from my hair color to my eye color to my size and my girth. This has no effect on my stats.

I decide to go with a hat for today, selecting it from a drop down menu that appears in the air before me. The benefits of a virtual entertainment dreamworld needn't be explained here – everything is accessible at my fingertips aside from freedom... aside from a way to log out of The Loop.

I chose a black military cap, tight, with a short brim. My blond hair grows out from underneath, styling itself. It isn't hard to look good in The Loop.

I kick open my door, just in case there's someone in the hallway waiting to ambush me. While the happenings around me are always the same, sometimes there is a surprise or two, which leaves me to believe that something is watching me, toying with me, cynically monitoring my cyclical existence. Possibly the NVA Seed, but I've long since given up my search for the world's puppet master.

The lights in the narrow hallway flicker.

Once, twice, three times, just like they always do. They stay off for twenty seconds and then come back on. Downstairs, something thuds and bangs; the next tag-team of palookas is here. A quick scroll through my inventory list and I decide to wing it this time.

There's nothing like a little hand-to-hand combat to jump-start my day.

~*~

Nonstop kicks. I arrive downstairs and reflect that five hundred and forty-six days is a long time to fight the same NPC thugs every morning. My avatar leaps into slow-motion as six John Does rush me all at once. My movement through the air is fluid, calculated, enhanced by my advanced abilities bar.

I'm good, dammit.

Think *The Matrix* meets Bruce Lee plus The Force if it helps to understand my capabilities in this VE dreamworld. Being in The Loop has its advantages, including the ability to break the laws of gravity and to flip the bird at the space-time continuum – at least until my advanced abilities bar depletes.

I'm in the air above the six assassins, my feet connecting with their skulls, volleying off one and thudding into the next. Kick-kick-kick go the feet and I don't even need an ice pick to take these NPCs goons out because they are much less effective than Morning Assassin– much, much less. I drop down behind the last of the six, cracking his neck backwards over my shoulder as he cries out, "Gor blimey!"

I turn to them and retrieve the .500 Magnum from my inventory list, item 466. Six blasts from the hand-howitzer later and someone better call the hotel's janitor. Smoking barrel, splattered bodies. One glance across the hotel lobby and I spot the NPC doorman cowering behind a potted plant.

"Morning Jim," I say. "Sorry about the mess."

"Good morning, Mr. Hughes. It's quite all right."

Jim stands slowly, straightening the front of his uniform. The dead look in his eyes indicate that he is playacting, that he is responding in an Non Player Character way to the violence he has just witnessed. What I wouldn't give to see some true human emotion, rather than the stereotypical, standardized response hacked up by an advanced algorithm, some regurgitated feeling, bird-vomited from one NPC to another.

"Please, call me Quantum," I tell him for the umpteenth time. "Are there any messages for me?"

There have never been any messages for me, but I always check anyway. After all, it's better to have hope in a hopeless place than to be hopeless in a hopeless place. Or something like that.

Trying to cajole, threaten, or torture information out of Jim has proven to be relatively fruitless. I generally leave him alone these days, greeting him before leaving in the morning and saying goodnight if I'm lucky enough to return in the evening. Sometimes I kill him just for the hell of it.

"No messages, sir," he says. He wipes beads of sweat from his forehead to the front of his pants, the sweating swine. *I should do something about him...*

I'm nearly out the door when Doorman Jim calls my name. "Mr. Hughes, I mean Mr. Quantum! There is one message, sir!"

"A message?" I turn to him. "Transfer it to my inventory."

The message appears in my inventory list, item number 546. I access it and read it twice.

Impossible.

"What is it, Mr. Hughes?"

"Please, call me Quantum."

"What is it, Mr. Quantum?"

I retrieve the S&W .500 from my list and shoot him in the neck.

"My apologies, Jim."

~*~

Violence is rewarded, or should I say, was rewarded in The Loop.

Doorman Jim is merely a daily casualty in The Loop, a virtual entertainment dreamworld that used to grade a person on how many people they killed that day. The higher your kill count, the higher you moved up on the Hunter List.

I was the top hunter the day The Loop began repeating itself, hence the reason everyone is after me. This is what makes me both anxious and excited to see a message from an actual person; or from whom I assume is an actual person. NPCs don't normally send messages. I read the message for the fifth time:

Quantum,

I've returned for you. Meet me in Devil's Alley as soon as you receive this.

Frances Euphoria

"Frances Euphoria?" I savor the name a few times, realizing that it's likely a trap.

It can't be a real person contacting me. Real people don't exist in The Loop, haven't for nearly two years. *Some group of randomly-generated NPCs is out to get me.* The thought of this makes me smile; at least it won't be a boring day.

One glance at the street confirms that it is dreary outside, as is every day in The Loop. The dreamworld was developed to cater to the Cyber Noir crowd, a niche market for those who like grit and tech, extreme violence, dark corners, sleuth-work, nineteen fifties styling with futuristic weapons. Cyber Noir was a subgenre that took off in the 2040s, at a time when Humandroid androids were replacing the workforce and governments were incorporating. Virtual entertainment dreamworlds, created through neuronal algorithms by the Proxima Company, became a swell way to escape, and I would still think they were a swell way to escape if I could find a swell way to escape this one.

The wind picks up, bouncing a tin can down the street. I don't even need to check the time. 8:17 AM, the minute of the tin can. It always stops directly in front of a vandalized trashcan, spins twice, settles.

Of course, I've tried a variety of different exit points from the hotel. I've leapt from rooftop to rooftop, sat and had coffee, slept in (after killing the morning assassin), and even gone room to room, trying to see if there were any clues that would free me from The Loop.

What I've discovered is this – every way out of my hotel has its own pre-determined history. If I go to the roof, lightning cracks in the sky above, connecting with an antenna on a building in the distance causing a beautiful spark. If I go room to room, I encounter a man snoring as a hooker in a garter belt steals his money. Both are NPCs, and I've killed them dozens of times in a variety of colorful ways.

If I have a cup of Joe and some pancakes courtesy of my main squeeze Dolly, a chef runs out of the hotel's kitchen at exactly 8:23 with a butcher knife trying to slice and dice me. (His meat cleaver marks day 123 in my inventory – it's great for hacking). If I sleep in, a different morning assassin comes at 9:29. If I sleep in past that, another one comes at 10:34.

And so on.

There is no escape from the repetitiveness of The Loop. This is why the message intrigues me so – it is a true break from the endlessly recurring nature of my Loop-life.

~*~

Reading the message for the seventh time doesn't give me any more clues regarding its origin.

And why does the person named Frances say *I've returned for you*? The only people that care about my condition are the ones keeping me alive in the real world; at least I assume there's someone keeping me alive up there. For all I know I may be nothing more than an imprint of consciousness, a ball of neuronal echoes that has outlived my human body.

My dreams say otherwise.

Almost every night I dream that someone is waking me; that someone is tending to me and taking care of me. If only this were true. If only The Loop was as forgiving as my dreams. Still, my dreams are equally suffocating. I can't wake up from them, no matter how hard I urge myself, no matter how hard I push myself forward in hopes of tearing from the virtual dream ether.

No matter how hard.

I raise my hand to hail a taxi. There are always taxis in The Loop, all sensuous curves and gaudy chopped and channeled black-and-yellow sheet metal, the cabs you'd see cruising the streets of 1940s New York City if R. Crumb had designed their taxis – except these taxis hover, just like the aeros vehicles in the real world.

A taxi always stops if you raise your hand in The Loop. They don't have preprogrammed histories like most of the other things that occur during my day. They only come when I want them to come. Of course, there are more interesting ways to travel in The Loop. If I wanted, I could pull an NPC driver out of their aeros, kill them, and take the aeros, but it's generally less hassle to travel peacefully. Besides, I'd like to make it to Devil's Alley in one piece.

A taxi lowers to the ground, its engine kicking and thumping. I get in and the driver turns to me. A huge grin nearly splits his phizog; a grimy bowler is jauntily cocked over one eye. "Where to, buddy?" He stinks of motor oil and tuna fish sandwiches.

"To the bowels of the city, Mac," I say. "And don't spare the horses."

"Devil's Alley, eh? You got it."

The engine coughs and sputters, catches, and blows fumes as we lift into the air. It doesn't need to cough and sputter and blow fumes, but everything here is designed to look old and beat up, scratched and dented, ripped and torn, used, abused, twisted,

14

cracked and crazed. Blemished, pockmarked, and polluted – the attributive adjectives of The Loop are endless. One glance at the seat's worn upholstery confirms this.

"What's buzzin', cousin?" the driver asks as he speeds along, weaving around other vehicles.

"You jivin' me, man?"

Sometimes I don't know if the NPC's are screwing with me or if they really don't know that I've been living the same day for nearly two years. I think Morning Assassin gets it, but the others…

"Jivin'? Whutchoo mean, jivin'?" he coughs, bangs his fist against his chest. The rain picks up and he flicks on his little windshield wipers; the digital water hits the windshield only to be whipped off by tiny wipers. There's something beautiful about it, but I'm too distracted by the driver's blabbering to really appreciate it.

"Hey, kid, I'm talking to you. Whutchoo mean?"

"I mean I live the same day every damn day. Why are we still talking?"

"If you want another hack jockey I can dump you out here…" He dips into a lower airlane.

I access my inventory list and snag item number 399 – a Taser. I press the button on the grip and electricity sparks and crackles in the back seat, a counterpoint to the lightning outside.

"Jesus!" the driver says, nearly swerving into another aeros in the opposite airlane.

"Goose it and can the chatter, Jack! And keep your eyes on the skylane you son of a bitch."

"All right, mister, keep your hair on – Sheesh!"

I enjoy the rest of the trip to Devil's Alley in relative silence. Once we've landed, I transfer credit to the driver, who is still angry I threatened him. Credit is used for most transactions in The Loop and I have an unlimited supply, pennies from heaven. No matter how much I spend, my account resets itself to the maximum amount every morning. Too bad there isn't anything I want to buy.

Devil's Alley is a big place, but I'm pretty sure Frances Euphoria will want to meet me at Barfly's, the most run-down, seediest, grimiest, blood-and-sawdust-on-the-floor gin joint The Loop has to offer. As I move deeper into the slum, NPCs gravitate towards me, clad in trench coats and fedoras, hiding their faces behind dark umbrellas. A streetwalker in a shiny red bomber jacket spins her umbrella behind her head like a tragic Madame Butterfly. A tranny diddles his ding-a-ling on the fire escape overlooking the entrance to the alley, while a cat hisses and a giant rat scurries through a mound of trash. Muscled kookies mill about shadowed doorways, cruisin' for a bruisin'.

I step into one of the alleys, over an NPC fiend shivering in the cold rain. A hand reaches out and latches onto my ankle.

"Hey brother…" the fiend cackles. "Can you spare some cred?"

I transfer him half of everything I have. "That should be enough to buy some Riotous."

The lights of the alley paint harshly contrasting diagonal stripes across his sallow, grimy face as he fumbles in his pocket. "You mocking me, smart guy?" he asks, pulling a switchblade. He twists the blade in the air like a drunken conductor. "You think you're better'n me, think you can just throw me cred like I'm some charity case!?"

16

The fiends in The Loop are vicious, unpredictable rat-bastards, a class of downgraded guttersnipes, slumdog tramps addicted to a drug known as Riotous. I press my finger into the air, accessing my inventory list. A drop-down menu appears in front of me; the bum freezes as I make my selection. Day 171's item will do the trick nicely. A sledge hammer appears in my hands and I swing it into his chest like I'm teeing off at the Apple Grove. He slams into the wall with a satisfying crunch of bone and cartilage, and blows pixelated blood out of his mouth and nose.

"Hey! You can't do that!" An even grungier fiend is on his feet, and I'm behind him before he can reach me. One swing of the sledge and he too Humpty-Dumptys into the muck and filth of the alley.

~*~

Barfly's sign buzzes and flickers at the end of the alley, a neon floozie in a Martini glass, endlessly scissoring her legs, electric bubbles popping above her head. People move through the shadows leading up to the place, speaking in whispers behind cupped hands, breathing in each other's cigarette smoke. Grit for breakfast, a kick in the teeth for lunch, home before dinner in a coffin carried by skeletal pallbearers, a .38 slug through your heart – welcome to my life. I've spent endless dismal days squatting in this dive, drinking to the point of faux-ossification and then fighting my way across The Loop, only to wake up back in the flophouse the following morning as if it had all been a dream.

Being bored is an understatement.

"Quantum." The doorman claps his arm across my shoulders. He is a chiseled guy, his face angular and rough like the Old Man of the Mountain's used to be, before it collapsed. This guy would give the Old Man a run for his money in the rustic mug department. Trust me, I know – I've dealt with Croc several times after things got dicey at Barfly's.

"I'll behave," I say instead of hello.

"You always do," he says with a flinty glint in his eye.

Maybe I'm spooked; maybe I've lived the same day so many times that there are surely things I haven't noticed in the 545 previous iterations. It kind of makes me wonder how much I missed when the days weren't on repeat, when The Loop (the name I've given it) was nothing more than the game-slash-entertainment dreamworld known as *Cyber Noir.*

"You waitin' on someone? Chippy, maybe?" Croc asks, chewing on a toothpick.

"You can tell? Some NPC you are… "

"NPC?"

Non Player Characters never refer to themselves as NPCs, which only makes this place more maddening. Sometimes I think I'm the crazy one… sometimes.

"Frail named Frances Euphoria. She here?" I ask. A quick scan across the bar tells me the usual suspects are present – drunks and divas, lounge lizards and booze hounds, gamblers, grifters and bunco artists – no matter what the clock reads. Getting soused is the name of the game.

"Frances Euphoria … "

"Well, Croc?"

"Don't know the broad. Pull up a pew and maybe she'll show. You never know, Daddy-O."

The patience flows out of his face and I oblige – no sense in riling this one up unnecessarily. I sit at the same barstool I always sit at, on the far left hand side of the bar, facing the door so I can see who comes in. One can only have a pool cue upside the noggin but so many times before one realizes that it may be time to change seats.

Cid the bartender is a grizzled old bastard in a white shirt, black bow tie, and none-too-clean apron, with a sawed off, lead-loaded baseball bat behind the bar. He pulls me a pint in a none-too-clean mug and slides it to me. I catch it before it sails off the end, and the exquisitely rendered foam slops over my hand. I savor the first swallow. It's cold-ish, and feels sort of beer-ish over my tongue, and if I pour enough down my piehole it'll get me kind of drunk-ish.

It ain't great, but it'll do.

I nod my thanks, and Cid winks in return. His mono-brow dances like a caterpillar on a hot plate.

A dame walks in, and she's the cat's meow – stacked like pancakes, with cleavage down to there and gams up to here, and a tight black dress that looks like it came out of a spray can. Her hair is devil red, her skin whiter than the finest blow, and the triangular icon over her head is blue – sky blue, cornflower blue, blue the color of life blue. She's an actual person, not an NPC, and I'm not going to lie – I'm simply mesmerized by the color. *Almost two years...*

"Frances Euphoria?" I wipe the beer foam off my lips.

"Three Kings Park, seven o'clock tomorrow night."

She turns slightly and she's all of a sudden sporting a *Crocodile Dundee*-sized Bowie knife with a brass cross-guard and stag scales. It's a well-crafted piece of steel, and I've got one just like it – item number 33 – in my inventory. She strikes like a cobra and slams the blade into my chest.

I'm dead before my pint hits the floor.

Day 547

Feedback sounds off in my skull. Digital Niagara, Rome as it falls. The sun fingers my eyelids as I swivel to the side, kicking my dirty blankets off. Ninjitsu disembark, no light before the dark.

The next day has come after being stabbed by Frances Euphoria at Barfly's.

My eyes trace across the walls of my not-so-ritzy hotel room. They are the color of earwax, stained from water damage, peppered with curious marks. A single painting depicting a sailboat fighting against a great storm hangs over my bed.

"Three Kings Park…" I mumble hoarsely.

My instinct tells me I have exactly four minutes until Morning Assassin's attack. I sit up, trying to recall the blue glow above Frances' head, the glow that indicated she was an actual person. *Imagine that.* Yesterday, I was killed by an actual person and just saying these words fill me with hope I haven't felt in ages. There are still other people, people who aren't controlled by algorithms. I would rejoice if there was time for celebration.

I access my inventory list midair, scrolling through my options. I have many ways in which to extinguish life, but I'm not feeling very creative today so I select a sawed-off shotgun, item 21. I lay in my bed, facing the window that Morning Assassin always bursts through. I'm surprised when I hear a knock-knock at my door at exactly 8:05.

"Who's there?" I ask, aiming my shotgun at the door.

"It's me."

"It's *me* who?"

The voice sounds familiar.

"Seriously? You're going to do this? It's *me!*"

"What do you want?"

"I want to talk to you – just talk."

"Jim?" It can't be the doorman, but there is no one else who would show up at this time aside from Morning Assassin.

"No, it's Aiden. C'mon, let me in. It's not like I don't already have a key anyway… "

Curiosity kills the avatar. "Okey-dokey, Smokey, but grab some air and keep 'em there."

The door opens and Morning Assassin strolls in like he owns the joint.

"Be cool. One false move and I'll ventilate ya," I say as I raise the shotgun.

He keeps his hands up. There is something different about him this morning, a strange melancholy I've never seen before. This tall drink of water is acting like he'd bet the farm on the trifecta and lost his winning ticket, Still, I smell a rat – he's been busting through the window for nearly two years trying to punch my ticket and now he just wants to chit-chat and chew the fat? Something ain't copacetic.

"Quantum." He nods his greeting. He's in a black jacket and big black kicks, like always. His black balaclava is shoved in his front pocket.

"Morning Assassin. You all of a sudden out of the morning assassin business or something?"

"I have a handle, you know."

"So does a toilet. What's your point?"

He rolls his eyes and makes the exasperated noise.

"Oh all right. What is it?"

"Aiden."

"I'll stick with Morning Assassin."

"Whatever floats your boat. It doesn't matter at this point anyway."

The way he says this makes me even more skeptical. "What's with the not breaking through the window like always?" I ask. "I was itching to murdalize you quickly this morning. Now you've come in here like a civilized NPC... tell me one reason why I shouldn't let daylight into your guts. One reason."

"I have a message for you."

I brandish my shooter and ready myself for his attack. "Go on... and keep 'em up, blockhead."

"Frances is dangerous... "

"*France* is dangerous? Maybe if you're a snail, but otherwise I don't see it."

He makes the noise of exasperation again. "No, *Frances* is dangerous; the broad – *Frances Euphoria.*"

"Frances Euphoria?" I lower my weapon. "How do you know about her?"

"She's dangerous, Quantum."

And then he changes.

23

Before I can react, he's all over me like a cheap suit, both fists come from over his head straight into my neck muscles, elbow in my schnozz, fist in my breadbasket, knee in my nuts. His surprise assault sweeps me backwards; I stumble like a rummy with a skin full of Sterno and my finger convulses against the trigger. Pain explodes in my groin; the front of my trousers is mass of bloody, ragged flesh. The only upside is that Morning Assassin caught a piece of it too, but not as bad – I don't think I've managed to shoot *his* dick off. Simulated shock and sudden blood loss grip me in an iron fist. The shottie slips from my grasp; the smell of burned gunpowder assails my nostrils like Satan's Burma Shave.

The Loop designers use a blurred, red-tinted viewing feed and the inability to access a new weapon from one's inventory list to indicate injury. The NV Visor I'm wearing in the real world – the world that I haven't seen in nearly two years – also triggers pain receptors through neuronal discharges. Things still hurt in The Loop, just not as bad as in real life, but the blurred vision and the inability to access one's inventory creates a horrifying sense of claustrophobia, as if one is truly trapped.

It's a question of whether or not I'll bleed out before Morning Assassin pounds me into smithereens. The smart money is betting on M.A. – he's got my empty shotgun now and he's wailing on me like I'm a red-headed step-child on a rented mule holding a piñata full of M&Ms at a fat kid's birthday party. M.A. knows what he's doing, so it doesn't last long – but it lasts long enough, and it hurts like hell. Finally, mercifully, at long last the lights grow dim, the fat lady belts one out.

"Hello darkness, my old friend, I've come to talk with you again... "

Day 548

Feedback until my eyes pry open. Feedback reverse lullaby, klaxon alarm clock cranial drone. My first thought upon opening my glims this morning is that I need to add an item to my inventory list to mark the passing of day 547. My next thought is I need to kill the shit out of the Morning Assassin for making me shoot myself and then beating me to death yesterday morning.

Baby steps to the violence.

Accessing my inventory list, I scroll as I decide the best way to get my revenge. Morning Assassin really did a number on me the previous day and I plan to do a number back. And what was with the warning about Frances Euphoria? What does M.A. actually know about her? I quickly make the decision to kill today and question tomorrow. Besides, I still need to meet her at seven o'clock tonight (I hope she's still there).

8:05 AM swings around and Morning Assassin shoulder- rolls into the room wielding a pair of nun chucks.

I'm still in bed, the blanket tastefully draped over me, my Chicago typewriter – item 247 – in my hands. I give him the Saint Valentine's Day treatment and he treats me to a Saint Vitus dance before he runs out of steam and hits the floor.

I kick the blanket off me and keep him covered as I add his nun chucks to my inventory list to mark the passing of day 547. Morning Assassin turns, groans, spits blood and tries to pull himself to his hands and knees.

I sneer as I deliver a .45 caliber love letter or three right in his ear. His lights go out like a candle in the wind, and he's thoroughly and completely dead – at least for today. The Thompson submachine gun – ain't nothing like it. I am trigger happy, hear me roar.

The 8:08 AM crow lands outside my window, watching me curiously. A dark cloud appears in the sky, covering the morning sun. Stepping over Morning Assassin's body, I stop in front of where the mirror used to be, which is now liberally sprinkled with bullet holes. I pick up the biggest piece of seven years" bad luck from the floor and look at myself. Geez Louise, my hollow eyes, my blondish-brown hair slicked over to the side, my pale skin; what do I look like in the real world now? I assume I'm in a dive vat in some digital coma ward somewhere, but there is really no telling.

My facial features morph as I scroll through a few avatar skins, eventually choosing blue eyes and a healthier complexion. Goodbye Goth, hello weekend on the boardwalk. I adjust the beard stubble to give me a stylishly hip five o'clock shadow. A zoot suit wraps me in its embrace: a killer-diller coat with a drape shape, reet pleats and shoulders padded like a lunatic's cell. Polished Italian leather dress shoes envelop my dogs. I button one of the buttons and smooth the front of the jacket with my hand as I admire the long gold watch chain.

I'd like to make a good impression before I kill Frances Euphoria later tonight.

~*~

Ten past eight.

I slip into the hallway outside my room and the lights flicker once, twice, three times. Every morning six assassins come to the hotel and every morning six assassins go home in algorithmic body bags. I select a flame thrower from my inventory – item number 83, an oldie but goodie – and strut to the stairwell ready to roast me some NPCs.

I slide down the railing just to be an asshole, just to make a grand entrance.

As soon as I hit the lobby, hellfire spews from the nozzle of my flame thrower, consuming the six droppers as I laugh maniacally for dramatic effect. Their limbs thrash and flail as their skin scorches, flesh flambés, and their brains broil. The smell of napalm in the morning tickles my nose but the smell of burning flesh is nonexistent – the designers didn't want to make it *too* real.

By 8:13, all that is left of the six assassins is a greasy pile of char and some scorch marks on the wall. I feel good today, suave in my suit and proud of my epic grandstanding. I turn to Jim the Doorman and bow.

"G-g-good… good morning, Mr. Hughes."

"Call me Quantum," I tell him.

"Right, Mr. Quantum."

"Any messages?"

"Ummmm… "

"Is that a yes or no, Jim?"

"There may be a message… but…"

"But what?"

Jim's eyes flicker red and his arm morphs into an enormous scythe blade.

"Yowza! Where did you get a mutant hack?"

I'm more curious than I am afraid. In the early years of Cyber Noir – The Loop – unscrupulous players developed mutant hacks to give them an unfair advantage in combat. They were quickly banned.

Before I can say anything else, Jim is on me like a pair of tighty whities. He almost separates me from my proboscis with his first swing of the scythe-arm.

"What gives?" I shout as I dodge his next attack. His peepers are the red of red hot chili peppers, his gob contorts in a grimacing downturned rictus. His movements are stiff, jerky – as if he's being controlled against his will. I can almost smell the fear radiating off him.

He comes at me again on the backswing, and I duck like Daffy. As soon as his scythe-arm passes, I access my inventory.

Accessing one's inventory is the best way to freeze a battle. It gives the player a moment to assess the situation, to quickly find a weapon to respond with. At least with NPCs it always has.

I can't give Jim a dirt nap; he's never attacked me before, which means something definitely isn't on the up-and-up. I'll need to deal with the big shiv before I can give him the third degree, so I select a chainsaw, item 112. The inventory screen disappears and Jim swings for the fence again.

"Do… not… meet… Frances… Euphoria!"

Each word escapes from his mouth as if it were forced, pushed from behind through his clenched teeth. His blade comes in low and I bend backwards at the knees, my upper body parallel to the ground. It whooshes by and clips the button from my coat. I bounce forward using my advanced abilities bar, and yank the cord on my chainsaw. It erupts into life on the first pull; the chain blurs into invisibility as the engine revs up.

Digital blood sprays onto my suit as I take his arm off at the shoulder. His scythe-arm hits the floor with a clang, twitches, lies still.

~*~

"Care to tell me what that was all about, Jim?" I ask the crawling doorman, who's leaving a calligraphic trail of blood behind him.

His head turns to me. "Don't … don't … "

"Jim, I consider you a friend, really I do, but you need to explain to me why you just tried to ice me with a mutant hack…"

His eyes dilate, become red again. He bares his teeth in a wolfman snarl as he says, "Do not meet Frances Euphoria." His voice drops an octave. "DO NOT MEET FRANCES EUPHORIA!"

"Well, Jim, I'm afraid that's what's on the agenda for today, and I'll be damned if I let an NPC doorman tell me what to do – it sets a bad precedent."

I quickly finish the job with my Kalashnikov, item 422, which I picked up at an off-the-books arms dealer over in The Pier.

With Jim dead and almost eleven hours to kill, I decide to have breakfast.

The chef will attack me at 8:23, so I dip into the kitchen and shoot the mustachioed little butterball with my Kalashnikov, a pre-emptive strike if there ever was one. I return to the dining area and Dolly the waitress appears. Her jet-black hair is bobbed and shiny, her eye-liner and mascara a la Cleopatra, her nails and lipstick stop sign red. She's in a black apron and a white blouse, a hotbody, fit and slender.

"What's cookin', good lookin'?"

I follow her eyes to my suit, which is covered in NPC blood. "Oops," I say. A new suit appears on my body instantly, freshly pressed and free from bloodstains.

"Good morning, Quantum. You're looking sharp today."

Dolly and I have been going steady for some time now. She never calls me Mr. Hughes and she has this very feline way of moving about the room, as if she knows I'm watching her every step. She's tall for a broad with a nice caboose and a classy chassis, who likes making out and giving massages. I'd say we hook up about three times out of seven, when I'm not in Devil's Alley at Barfly's, or slaying maggots at The Pier. I am a magnet for maggots.

"Say, what's the scoop with Jim the Doorman?" I ask.

"What do you mean?"

NPCs don't usually acknowledge the death of other NPCs unless they've personally witnessed it. Still, I figured a question was worth asking. "He came at me this morning…"

"I don't know nothing about it," she says just a shade too quickly.

" … and he did it with a mutant hack."

Her eyes dart down to her order pad. "Don't know nothing about that, either."

"Hey, you ever heard of a dame name of Frances Euphoria?" I ask casually.

She looks away, equally casually. "Nope, doesn't ring a bell."

"What's the word on the street then? Anything I should know about?"

"You writing a book or something?"

Her voice is sultry, smoky, honey to my ears.

"You reading one?"

"Quit teasing, Quantum, you know I'm working." She bats her eyes at me and my heart twists into a knot.

"Baby, you're always working."

Dolly shakes her order pad at my face. "Come on big spender, what do you want? I don't got all day."

"What, you got an appointment or something? "

"Yeah," she says playfully, "with a classy millionaire crime-fighter." The wink and the accompanying crooked grin makes my cyber-pulse pound.

"Well, if he can't make it, how about a little snooze in my room. What do you say? How about 4:30? A little shut-eye never hurt nobody."

"I don't know … " By her tone of voice I know she knows she'll be there. I decide not to press the point.

"I'll have my usual then."

"Eggs over easy, three pieces of toast, bacon and a beer?" she asks, scribbling away on her order pad. 'sound about right to you?"

"Sounds about right. Let me get a plate of pancakes too, extra butter. I got a long day ahead of me."

"Pancakes it is, sweetie, extra butter."

The food comes and boy it is beautiful. The grease is still sizzling on the bacon; the eggs are glazed, the yolks unbroken; there are squiggly grill lines on the toast; the pancakes are perfectly round, golden brown at the edges. Too bad I can't actually taste the food.

Food in The Loop has no flavor, produces no energy nor is there any point in eating it. I eat simply to remember what it was like *to* eat. I eat simply to go through the motions of eating; I eat to remind myself that somewhere I have an actual body that is currently being nourished through a feeding tube.

Sounds, smells and visuals are ever-present in The Loop due to the Neuronal Visualization Visors – NV Visors – that users wear back in the real world. The visor developers never got the taste mechanism right, but for all I know they may have been perfected by now – two years is a long time for technology to progress.

I down my beer and ask for another.

"You're getting started early," Dolly says with a wink. "A real trooper, you are."

"What can I say? Is there a better way to fire up your engines in The Loop?" Of course, I can't get drunk, but I can at least pretend I'm drunk.

"Let me know if you need anything else, Quantum."

"See you at 4:30, Doll."

Dolly swivels away from me, moves real slow back to the kitchen so I can watch her depart.

~*~

I stumble up to my room and check the time. An assassin should be here any moment now.

The bullet holes from earlier are gone, as is the shattered window and broken mirror. The physical environment of The Loop resets itself periodically. I could use my grenade launcher – item 35 – to blast a crater-sized hole in my wall and it would be fixed by the time I returned from the lobby downstairs. I find this slightly unsettling – while everything is grimy in the rat trap that is The Loop, the fact that the environment quickly repairs itself nullifies the filth, constantly reminding me that this is all prefabricated, nothing more than an advanced algorithm. For once I'd like to see a bullet hole last for more than an hour. For once...

I access item number 520, a bear trap, which I recently picked up at The Pier. After I set the trap, I hide a landmine – item number 72 – directly next to it. That should do the trick.

Once the trap is set, I get in bed and watch the digital rain plink against the window. Lightning cracks in the sky and thunder rumbles like a giant's belly after a plate of stewed Englishman. The sound of thunder is eventually annoying. It's supposed to be randomly generated, but it too is stuck on a loop that repeats itself every five minutes. It took me a while to notice it, maybe a hundred and fifty days, but the repetitive thunder sounds have irked me ever since.

Like clockwork a goon breaks through the window, sort of Morning Assassin Lite. He lands in the bear trap, which slams shut and triggers the landmine, tearing his NPC body to shreds.

The blast radius is controlled, although it shouldn't be, by a hack I installed before the days started repeating themselves. The hack makes it so that I can't be injured by the explosives I set, something that has come in handy multiple times, like right now.

The smoke clears. All that is left of the man is a blackened hole in the ground rimmed with blood. I can see the floor below me through the hole, and get the urge to explore the room simply to kill time. Upon lowering myself to the floor below, I find a child sitting on the bed clutching a pillow.

A lone child generated in a hotel room in The Loop? Something's hinky here – there's never been anyone in this room before.

I quickly access my inventory and select the nun chucks, item 547. I might as well test them out. My list disappears and the ankle-biter begins to sob. "What's the beef, chief?" I ask, the nun chucks behind my back.

"My mommy left me here…" he sobs.

"My mommy left me here too, kid, but you don't see me getting all boo-hoo about it."

I'm seconds away from cracking the little germ on the head with my chucks when he looks up at me and asks, "Can you help me? P-p-please?"

"Help you what?"

"Find my mommy… "

"Where are you from, kid?"

"I live in The Badlands."

"Which part?"

He says, "Near Devil's Alley with my mom and my uncle. He has a problem."

"What kind of problem?"

"My uncle's not like the others… "

"None of us are."

The yoot sure knows how to tug a heartstring. He's an NPC and he doesn't have a real mother, nor does he have a real uncle. My brain tells me this, but my heart takes in his oval eyes and his tear-stained cheeks and the fact that he's all alone, stuck in a hotel room somewhere without his mother and my heart *nearly* overcomes my better judgment.

Nearly.

"Sorry kid, you're on your own."

I turn to the door, ignoring his sobs. I need to stay alive today. It's hard enough to make it to seven o'clock without going on some hide "n' seek adventure with some kid to find his mommy.

I'm just about to turn up the stairs towards my room when I hear some moaning in room 202. One solid boot to the door later and I find a bald guy with an ugly gut reaming some older broad with dyed blonde hair.

"Hey buddy!" he says, turning his ugly face my way. He resembles one of the taxi drivers in The Loop, jowly and grody. "You mind closing the door? I'm busy here!"

The thought of killing them both crosses my mind. They are, after all, in *my* hotel and what's worse, they appear to be randomly generated just like the kid, which leads me to believe that something *really* isn't right in The Loop, as if I'm being tested. They freeze mid-hump as I access my inventory list and select the sawed-off shotgun, item number 21.

Lightning cracks outside as my list dematerializes.

"Hey!" the man says as soon as he's looking down the barrel of my shottie. Clickety-BOOM, Clickety-BOOM. And just like that, digital blood is Jackson Pollocked on the headboard. I'm just about to turn around when I hear a sob behind me.

"Mommy?"

I turn to find the little NPC crumbsnatcher clutching his pillow, staring in horror at the two bloodied corpses lying on the bed.

"It's for your own good, kid."

I raise my shotgun. Clickety-BOOM.

~*~

The floor and the wall in my room have repaired themselves; everything is in its right place.

I feel no remorse for what I've done to the kid, his mother and the cabbie pounding her. To kill is to be part of The Loop; the name of the game is maim. It's why I was the top hunter before the days began repeating themselves. There is no room for guilt, compassion, or mercy inside a virtual entertainment dreamworld. The weak sisters don't last long.

I relax onto my bed, waiting for the next assassin to arrive. He should be here in less than an hour, at 10:34.

As I wait, my mind tries to piece together little slivers of my memories of the real world. What does it feel like to taste something? To breathe fresh air? To hold someone's hand? To know that you *can* die, that your life can be quickly extinguished by a nuanced mistake?

My eyes open, settling on a pack of smokes on the nightstand. I reach out for the due backs, only to remember I've saved a cigarette in my inventory to mark the passing of day 545. I decide to smoke this cigarette instead, as it will replenish itself by tomorrow. The coffin nail appears in my mouth, conveniently pre-lit. After a long drag, a perfectly pixelated cloud of digital carcinogens materializes in front of me.

Back to the real world. Will I ever go back? Will I ever know what it's like to truly exist? And what of the real world, the world into which I was born? How has it changed? What's become of the place in the two years I've been trapped inside The Loop?

My mother. Her face comes to me, crow's feet in the corner of her eyes, her skin aged but glowing, her hair fair and curled at the ends, white on top and brown on bottom. She was the one who named me Quantum against my dad's better wishes. "Quantum is a futuristic name. The future begins anew every morning," she was fond of saying.

How was she? Was she still alive? Was she sitting in a hospital next to my body right now? For that matter, how was I being kept alive? Who was taking care of me? Who was making sure I didn't die trapped in the algorithmic dreamscape that is The Loop? And to add to this, was I already dead?

Feedback. It starts slowly, bathing me in its cantankerous jittering, neural calm sputtering. It sounds like someone has sliced off my ears and taped them to the sides of a rainmaker. The feedback is all-encompassing, all powerful and furious.

The sound of my entrapment is something I'll never grow used to.

~*~

Fast forward to 4:30. I've killed nine assassins in creative ways since the start of the day and haven't done much else. A single knock at my door and Dolly enters in a strapless red gown. She smells fresh, as if she's just come from the spa. Her skin is radiant, healthy, damn near translucent. Drop dead gorgeous.

"Dolly," I purr, all Rico Suave. "I thought you'd never arrive."

She sits on the corner of my bed, looking at me over her naked shoulder. "Why the fancy threads?" she asks.

"Oh, this old thing?" I shrug. "Sometimes a boy just wants to look nice. Anything wrong with that?"

"No... " She scoots up until we are both sitting with our backs against the headboard. Rain taps lightly against the window outside, separating us from the gloom of the city. Her arms cross in front of her gown, lifting her breasts in a way that kick starts my engine. "You meeting someone?"

"No."

"'Then why are you all dressed up? You got a hot date or something?"

"You're my hot date, doll face. Why d'you ask?"

"Just curious."

"Long day?" I ask her, changing the subject.

"Long enough."

The strangest thing about our relationship is the fact she never recognizes that she's an NPC, that she's essentially a string of ones and zeros that has a sexual relationship with a human player marooned in her world. She doesn't realize that each day is the same, nor does she ever make mention of our previous encounters. While her actions can't be exactly timed like those of the other NPCs and objects in The Loop, they are still predictable. I go for breakfast. We arrange to meet at 4:30. She arrives in a red dress – this is our routine.

"What about you?" She tucks her head under my chin. "How was your day? You just lounging around all day?"

"Playing it safe. I have places to go and people to see and I'd rather not die before I can get that squared away."

"'De?" Her laugh is bizarre, unusual, not at all the cheerful, tinkly music it always is. "You big lug, why are you so worried about dying? You seem healthy to me… " She dips her chin and looks at me through lowered lashes. "You feel like showing me how healthy you are?"

"You do know that…" I am about to remind her that she is an NPC and I'm a human when I decide to keep my mouth shut. These types of discussions never end well between us. "We should catch a flick sometime," I say, just to say something.

"I'd like that, Quantum."

"I could borrow a flip-top and we could head to the old drive-in cinema near Three Kings Park. A little back seat bingo… "

She play slaps. "Behave… "

"Come on, Dolly, it would be fun. Nothing wrong with a visit to the old passion pit."

"Stop it, you're embarrassing me. You know I have to work at night."

Dolly reaches back, undoes the hooks, and the top of her gown falls away. She really is a superbly rendered example of a higher order female mammal. Her arms fold in front of her breasts to preserve her modesty, and she shivers slightly.

"You cold?"

"Getting there," she says.

"I can tell."

My stylish garments go back to their digital clothes rack as her arms go around my neck. She presses against my chest, round and warm and firm. I kiss her cheek, her ear, wishing that she was a real woman, that we could have real sex, not some simulated version where anything goes and yet nothing does – there's no release, no relief, no real reward.

My best gal in this never-ending hell-hole lies back and welcomes me with open arms... and open legs. I take a moment to savor this simulated vision of loveliness. She's stacked, but skinny – not bad skinny, but bend-me-every-which-way-skinny, and she puts her ankles on my shoulders and her nails in my back. She moans low and sweet and sultry, urging me on, "Oh, come on baby, come on – fill me, thrill me. Oh, come on honey, come on and do me like you do!" as she showers my face in kisses.

Oh Dolly, I'd love to; I wish I could, but it just doesn't happen here in The Loop. Well, it does, but not like it does in real life; here it's a shadow of a shadow – Diet New Coke instead of Jolt Cola, a kiss on the cheek from your sister instead of tonsil-hockey with the slutty cheerleader. It's not *unfun,* and it's better than nothing, but it still ain't the real thing.

Our movements synchronize as she rakes her nails down my back, slides her gams down and around and clenches me tight. I hammer her towards the inevitable, unsatisfying conclusion.

"Oh, Quantum, oh honey baby darling, Oh come on, my rodeo rider, make it happen, Oh. Baby, Take Me THERE! Oh yes, oh yes, OH YES YES YES!"

Oh No!

Out of the corner of my eye I detect motion that shouldn't be there; the world freezes around me as I access my inventory list. Dolly's eyes are crazy orange, her lips a berserker's snarl, her hand full of item number 33. I'm really starting to hate that big, bad, bone-handled Bowie.

I select a fire extinguisher, item number 299, and I shift my leg to the left as soon as the inventory list disappears. Her knife swipes left as I lean out of the way and avoid the blade. I hammer the fire extinguisher into her face, again and again, hating myself in the process, hating the fact that I'm bashing her to death.

"Why Dolly?" I ask. "Of all people, why you?"

I'm on my feet in a matter of moments, waiting for her to come back to life, for her to attack me again. Her arm lifts and falls onto the bed; the small indicator above her head turns red, announcing her NPC death. I trusted Dolly more than I trusted anyone else inside this godforsaken virtual entertainment dreamworld. She has never tried to attack me before, never shown me any sign of animosity.

Now this.

"DAMMIT!"

Her bloodied head on my pillow and the knife on the ground sends a bolt of fury through my avatar. "Dammit!" I scream, tossing the nightstand over. I walk over to the window and punch it until it shatters, until my knuckles are covered in blood and my life bar has dropped a few notches. The thunder on repeat outside and the sharp rain only makes me that much angrier.

"Dammit!"

The painting of the sailboat comes off the wall, and I break it against my knee. I access my tommy gun from my inventory, item 247, and fill my wardrobe with bullet holes. My hands come to the splintered wood and I tear it apart piece by piece, tossing the pieces over my shoulder.

Next is the mirror. I slide over to the mirror and punch my reflection until it is blood-soaked, watery and vulgar. My knees come to my chest as soon as I sit on the floor sobbing.

Damn The Loop, damn the infinite violence. One glance to my bed reminds me of what I've just done, what Dolly has just attempted to do. Dog eat dog world, but I'm not an animal. I... Dolly is all I have here and now she's trying to kill me too! My one escape, the one thing I enjoyed about my existence has just turned cold and deadly and horrible, and all I can do is sob miserably as lightning cracks outside and the water-stained walls in my room constrict, reminding me of just how trapped I truly am.

"Get it together, Quantum," I say, slapping my hand against the side of my face. "Get it together."

~*~

I'm over it.

Eventually it's time for me to hail a taxi to Three Kings Park. I could walk there, but that would unnecessarily expose me to a variety of NPC hardcases, who would more than likely try to kill me. The day has been strange; The Loop's repetitive nature is altering for some reason, and it freaks me out. *Dolly tried to kill me.* Nearly two years of the same thing every day and finally – finally – things begin to change. This is what's upsetting me; this is what urges me to be more cautious than usual.

I've forgotten what it feels like to wake up, to pull myself out of reverie and take that first gasp of morning. Waking up. What I wouldn't give to somehow rip myself free from this virtual dreamworld, stretch myself thin until I reach a breaking point. Who would be there to celebrate? My mother? My father? In the real world I exist somewhere – at least I think I do – but here I'm nothing. Here I'm essentially dead.

Outside the hotel glaring at the streets now. My hand goes up and a taxi shoots down from the sky. The back door pops open and I get inside.

"Three Kings Park."

I don't even look at the driver this time, so focused I am on the thoughts that plague me.

"You got it, ace."

The cab lifts into the air and I settle into the torn upholstery. The city of bedlam and deceit that is three parts Gotham and one part Hell's Kitchen, swells all around me. The landscape of The Loop is defined by jagged edges, cathedral spires in the distance and gargoyles glowering down from impossibly high buildings, dead gardens atop crusty apartment blocks and leafless trees with mangled branches. Sin city sullied biome. To say

I hate it here is an understatement. To say I can't imagine myself anywhere else is also an understatement.

"Got the blues, bud?" the driver asks. He turns on the radio and a BB King track punctures the silence. King's fingers gracefully scrape up the neck of the guitar, pinching sound waves in a way that no one has ever been able to emulate.

"I got nothing," I say, thinking of what it was like to kill Dolly. The fact that she'll respawn only adds to my agitation. Born to try and kill me again. And me – here I thought we actually had something going on, that I was actually having a relationship with software, an algorithm. Is there any difference between this relationship and the relationships people have with Humandroids back in the real world? No idea. It's been so long since I've been in touch with the real world.

"You got nothing?" the driver laughs. "Sounds to me like someone is having a bad day."

"You can call it that. Better, you could call it a series of bad days, 548 bad days to be exact," I growl.

"Huh?" His bushy eyebrows furrow in the rearview mirror as he looks me over. "I don't read you, ace. Whutchoo you mean?"

"Nothing. Turn the music up."

~*~

Three Kings Park.

The place is the vomit trough of the city, long since abandoned, desolate and shit-tacular. The sandboxes are filled with broken glass, most of the swings hang from one chain, the basketball court has been stripped bare, the trees are overgrown, alive but dead in their own way. Portions of the benches have been torn to shreds, making it damn near impossible to sit.

Night has already settled by the time I arrive. The only light in Three Kings Park comes from a couple of trash bins spewing flames. NPC bums stand around the bins warming their hands, drinking fortified wine, freebasing Riotous as they speak in garbled voices. Mindless chatter – two words that couldn't be more apropos.

"Thanks," I tell the cabbie. After I've transferred the fare to the driver, his taxi lifts into the air.

I kick through a pile of dry leaves as I make my way towards the center of the park. A broken rake reveals itself; I add it to my inventory list to acknowledge day 548. I don't know where Frances Euphoria plans to meet me, but I figure the center will be a good place to start. I walk along a darkened path, through tendrils of smog, ignoring the digital crows squawking in the trees. A bottle hits the ground somewhere near the entrance; the sound of shattering glass reminds me that I'd better have a weapon ready just in case.

My inventory list appears in front of my face and I scroll through it, wondering what I should select. I could go with the mini-gun, item 198, but the weight makes it difficult to move quickly. My finger runs across a pair of throwing stars, item 315, and from there I scroll back to a PHASR (Personnel Halting and Stimulation Response), item 108, which is the weapon used by the US Department of Aggressive Defense during their various freedom initiatives. The PHASR features a neuromuscular inhibitor which may prove useful, especially if I need to interrogate Frances Euphoria before I kill her.

The PHASR appears in my hands.

It is massive, about the length of a baseball bat. The end is rounded off, topped by a cube-shaped exit point. I select the neuromuscular inhibitor, keeping one hand on the trigger and the other on the forestock.

A pavilion in the center of the park comes into view. A single figure stands in the pavilion, her form barely visible in the fog. A blue triangular icon over her head indicates that she is indeed human.

~*~

"Hands up," I say as I approach Frances Euphoria.

The sky coughs up a small drizzle; lightning cracks overhead; a cat screeches somewhere; a murder takes place behind a bush – the shit hits the fan.

"Quantum."

Her red hair frames her face like a bullseye. It is the only color in the park aside from the flames burning along the park's perimeter. An actual person is in front of me, her eyes clear, the indicator above her head telling me that Frances truly is human, a real *live* human. Her blue life bar appears in the corner of my eye, something that only happens with human players. The tingling sensation one feels as a prequel to crying comes to me. I can't tell if it is happening to me in The Loop or in the real world – am I coming through? Am I actually feeling a real emotion?

"Quantum."

I raise my weapon. There is no better way for me to interpret the turmoil I'm feeling than violence.

46

"Remember?" she asks.

I squeeze the trigger, snarling as a purple zap from my PHASR washes over Frances Euphoria. The beam dissipates, fizzing into the background. Shields aren't allowed in The Loop, which means she must have some sort of mutant hack.

"What are you?" I ask as I silently switch my PHASR to rapid-fire mode. I look down to my trembling hands. "Why did you kill me last night!?"

The feeling of violence overcomes the sense of loss rippling through me. I blast her again with my PHASR. The three rapid-fire shots slap into her shield and deflect, connecting with the pillars of the pavilion.

"Relax, Quantum," she says, and the voice is almost motherly, a tone that indicates that she knows I can't help myself, I can't suppress the fury tunneling through my veins. "I killed you because the NVA Seed was monitoring my actions. It was my only option."

"What are you!?" I ask. "Why…" Better words come to me, stronger and more accurate. "Why are you here? Who the hell are you? Who!?"

"Easy, easy, Quantum," she says. "I'm about to tell you something that will be hard for you to process."

I raise my weapon and select LASER, even though I know it will have no effect.

"How long have you been here in The Loop?"

"For… 548 days, today," I manage to say.

"No."

Now that the initial shock of meeting her has waned, I take in what she's wearing – a black combat uniform with a small popped collar, a sash filled with small leather pouches across her chest, a pair of knee-high boots with two-inch heels. "You've been here much longer than 548 days," she says. "Much longer."

"How long?"

"You really don't remember anything do you?"

"What am I supposed to remember?" I nearly scream. "One moment I was in the game, the next I couldn't log out! I contacted the administrators multiple times – nothing. I began keeping track of the days by putting a single item in my inventory list for every day that passed. So far, 548 days have passed, give or take a few... " I keep mumbling for another minute until she stops me.

"You've forgotten so much," she says to herself.

"What do you mean?"

"What day do you think it is in the real world?"

"I think it is... " My hand comes in front of me and I access my calendar. "It is nearly 2052. I lost the ability to log out in 2050, January 31st. I know for a fact."

A floating screen appears in front of her and she scrolls through her login details. With the twist of her wrist, the screen turns to me and I see a clock timed to the second. Above the clock is a date: May 15th 2058.

"2058? Impossible!" I raise my weapon and fire. It zips over her shoulder, connects with one of the trees surrounding the pavilion. The tree explodes into flaming splinters.

"Quantum, you have been stuck in C.N. for nearly eight years."

"The Loop! It's called The Loop!"

"No, that's what *you* call it. The world is, well was, called Cyber Noir, CN for short. It's one... one of many worlds in the Proxima Galaxy."

I know this, but the fact that she has essentially shattered my world makes me angry, confrontational. She freezes as soon as I access my inventory. I quickly select a serrated hand ax – item 96 – that I picked up at Barfly's one night. If a directed energy weapon can't blast through her shield, perhaps ignorance, anger, and brute force will yield tangible results.

My inventory screen disappears.

"You've chosen an ax?" Her red lips part to say something else.

"What do you want from me!?" I ask. "You come here and disrupt my life... my... "

But I hate my life! Confusion settles in and I have no idea what I should do. I swing at Frances Euphoria; her hand comes up and she catches the sharp end of my ax between thumb and forefinger.

"What the... ?"

It's been so long since I fought an actual human in The Loop that I've forgotten they too have advanced abilities.

"You can't kill me," she says, pinching the ax blade. I feel my arm tense up. *What is she doing?*

I've used my left hook numerous times to take my opponents off guard. Unfortunately, Frances Euphoria isn't a normal opponent. She stops my fist with a single finger. Circular waves form around my closed fist as I press forward, testing her immense power. The waves grow in size and intensity until they surround both of our bodies.

"Quantum, you can't kill me... "

Draining my advanced abilities bar, I press forward, hoping to throw her off guard.

Whud!

Her forehead flattens my nose in a Liverpool kiss and I fly into a support pillar of the pavilion, smashing through it. My life bar is half-full now, which should be impossible – I've leveled my avatar up to a point where hand-to-hand contact rarely has any effect on my hit point.

"Are you done?" she asks. "Are you ready to talk?"

Frances Euphoria floats over me now like some sort of banshee, her red hair beating in the wind, accented by sharp cracks of lightning in the darkened sky. I raise my hand to access my inventory list.

I'm dead before my list can even appear.

Day 549

Feedback my poisonous mistress, damn your whisperings in my ear, your constant barrage on my consciousness. Let me sleep, damn you! Let me never wake up again in The Loop! Let me rest in peace! The sun daggers my eyelids and I know exactly where I am, the place I'll eternally awaken in, the place that has come to define my cursed existence.

The Loop.

Groggy feedback pours out of my ear forming a silver puddle on my bed. I stir my finger in the puddle, tracing the name of the woman who has killed me twice now – Frances Euphoria. The hopped up female avatar must be destroyed. I don't know why she is here, but something isn't right and only I can get to the bottom of it.

Morning Assassin will be here any moment now. I scroll through my inventory list, looking for the perfect way to slaughter-start my day. The meat cleaver – item 123 – could do, but that would require effort and I really don't feel like a long, arduous squabble. The bear trap plus landmine combo seemed to do the trick the previous day. I select both items and set the trap.

8:05 rolls around and the Morning Assassin doesn't come.

I wait three more minutes for the crow to appear. *It doesn't.* Black clouds have yet to form in the sky outside, no thunder either. In fact, the sun is actually shining, which is bothersome because the only time it has shone in the last 548 days is for the first five minutes of the day.

I pull up my stats, clicking on the calendar, gasping when I see the date and time. May 16th 2058, 8:09:19 AM.

"Shit… "

Is it possible? Has The Loop stopped repeating itself?

I step into the hallway without checking my reflection in the mirror. I'm in my zoot suit, as I was when I was killed last night, and changing clothes is way down on the list of things that require my attention this AM. My head turtles out of my door, to the lights in the hallway.

They don't flicker.

The six assassins should appear downstairs at 8:12, their entrance marked by something falling on the floor. My inventory list appears and I select a baseball bat, item 17, for my left hand and a katana, item 155, for my right hand.

I listen for the sound that signifies their entrance. *Nothing.* I check the time – 8:13. I wait through another two minutes of unadulterated silence, ready to go full throttle.

My God, what is going on here? I'm almost too panicked to move down to the lobby. Change is unsettling; routine is what drives humanity.

As jittery as a jive-ass junkie on a jolt of Drano doesn't begin to describe how I feel at the moment, as Jim the Doorman greets me at the bottom of the stairs.

"Mr. Hughes, you have a guest."

I spin, bringing the bat against the back of Jim's head while simultaneously driving the katana into his kidney.

A slow clapping greets me. "Bravo, Quantum. Very *Iron Knight, Silver Vase*."

I unsheath the katana from Jim's corpse, whirl to face the voice, and hold myself ready. I peer across the lobby to find Frances Euphoria sitting on a worn leather couch with her legs crossed.

"We really need to talk."

~*~

"Turn your body shield off," I growl. "Fight me!"

"Sit down and stop being so hostile. If you would relax for a minute, you'd realize I'm here to help you." Frances Euphoria is in her black uniform with her hair framing her long neck.

"Help me?" I aim my sword at her, twist it slightly. "How are you going to help me? You've killed me twice and somehow... somehow you've managed to change the layout of my day. What have you done? Tell me, dammit!"

"The NVA Seed modified it, not me. I have nothing to do with this, or the glitch, or the fact that you can't log out."

"Are you some type of administrator?" I ask, ignoring what she has just said. "There aren't any human players in The Loop, haven't been for almost two years."

"Eight years. I am not an administrator, but administrator privileges granted to my position allow me to have thing such as mutant hacks."

"Your position?"

An explosion rocks the kitchen, rattling the ground. I glance up at the ceiling and watch the chandelier above Frances snap off its chain. She zooms out of the way before it flinderizes the sofa.

"They're here… " Frances now stands a few inches away from the fallen chandelier. "Come with me if you want to live."

"Why should I trust you?"

"I'm here to save you!"

"Yeah, you keep saying that, toots."

Four avatars with the blinking blue triangle of a live user stride through the lobby's newest entrance. And… what a surprise – virtually identical big, bulky ersatz road warrior wannabes in their fantasy biker-Viking black leather and chain mail, bedazzled with teeth and bones and spikes and all the usual wowsie-wow tough-guy accoutrements. They've even got skull masks with fangs and horns, straight from a Predator's wet dream. I've seen guys just like these a thousand times before and I'm all *ho-hum*.

Frances seems to be taking them seriously though, and maybe I should too, but c'mon, it's like *Mad Max* is calling and *Thunderdome* wants its costumes back! Once, just once I'd like to see someone show up with fairy wings, tutu and a magic wand. Now *that* player I'd take seriously. I look at them and cough, *"Dickless! Dickless!"* into my fist.

"We found them," one of the men says.

Frances gives me the hairy eyeball. "Get behind me, Quantum." A light twists around Frances Euphoria's arm. "These men can actually kill you… in real life."

~*~

One of the them steps forward. He is clearly the leader, evident in his stance and demeanor. He's hooded like the others, but the bottom of his mask is broken, revealing the makings of a beard. Sharp teeth from the mask cover his blackened lips.

"Release Quantum to us and you can go." His voice is metallic, as if he were speaking through a mechanical larynx.

"Why are you in C.N.?" Frances asks. "Go back to the main portals. There are better places to deal in death."

"You know why we're here," he says.

I slowly bring my hands behind my back, hiding my baseball bat and katana. They de-materialize as I return them to my inventory list. With my hand out of sight, I quickly scroll through my weapons stash, which momentarily freezes the action. I do this as quickly as possible.

If I remember correctly, and I do, players can switch weapons during a battle with another human player. This pauses gameplay for the person changing weapons, placing an hourglass over them that all can see. Accessing items in battle is dangerous because the person *not* scrolling through their inventory can move to a position of significant advantage in relation to the player on pause and shank them in the spleen, or something equally insalubrious before the paused player unfreezes.

Luckily, I know exactly which weapon I need: mini-gun, item 198. It's in my hand less than a second later, pointed at the four Chucklebutts. The feed chute snakes over my shoulder to the thousand-round ammo backpack.

"A mini-gun?" one of them asks. He laughs, a hoarse, throaty guffaw made worse by his metallic voice box.

The mini-gun spins up and I pull the trigger before he can finish laughing.

A solid stream of flying hate roars into laughing boy; he splatters like he's been smacked with the Mystic Mallet Mjolnir, and splashes onto the other three who flinch away and return fire with their assault rifles.

"Dammit Quantum!" Frances Euphoria tosses a small metal ball in front of me. It goes *zzzzt!* and emits a green grid that wraps around me like a fat Auntie's hug. Incoming bullets spang off me and my life bar doesn't deplete – deflector shield, ha-HA!

Frances' arm morphs into a shotgun with twin barrels the size of mortar tubes. I've never seen this mutant hack before, but I hardly have time to be impressed. Her blast chews the arm and shoulder off the nearest leather boy, who goes down, squealing like a perforated porcine and then disappears when the player logs out.

"Holy Frijoles, Batman!" I shout, as she blows another one into cat food with her double barrel arm howitzer.

The leader's arm morphs into a wicked, jagged blade with an underslung gun barrel, similar to the weapon Frances is wielding. He comes at her fast, much faster than I can move – which is saying something – and she parries his blade with her über-gun.

They fly around the lobby like Andy Capp and Flo, like Roadrunner and Wile E. Coyote, like the Tasmanian Devil in a Texas Twister on crack, faster than the NV visor can render or the mind can follow. Wherever they touch explodes into shards and flinders, smoke and noise; they shoot and miss, shoot and miss; blast gaping holes in the very fabric of the lobby and I wonder if they'll bring the building down. I am rendered impotent by their speed; they are hummingbird fast and phorusrhacid deadly. All I can do is stand there like Cletus Spuckler in slack-jawed amazement.

And then it's over; the leader's head spins across the lobby, his body hits the floor and shatters into a million pixels.

I turn to find Frances Euphoria panting, holding her double-barreled mutant hack with her other hand. Two katana blades retract into the gun while some heart-like organ pulsates on the side of her weapon, its beating slows as the mutant hack shrivels.

"They've found us," she announces with a grimace.

"They who? What now?"

"We need to get someplace else NOW, before word gets out."

"Barfly's?" I ask. "I'm craving a morning pick-me-up."

~*~

The sun is still in the sky, accenting The Loop in a way I haven't seen in years. I can see for miles on end from the window of our taxi, over the gothic spires of abandoned churches, through the legs of rusted water tanks, around all the sharpened corners of shady clip joints and hidden stash spots. I can even see the perimeter of the city, a place known as The Badlands. It's a cliché name for a place that essentially spells the end of the VE dreamscape that is The Loop.

All Proxima Worlds have an end or a border that has the ability to transport you to the opposite end of the map. This is akin to circumnavigating the globe and, years ago when I wasn't stuck in The Loop, reaching a map's border was the best way to travel to the other side. In worlds that required credit to travel, one could simply walk to the nearest border and be instantly transferred to the corresponding side.

The Loop has no such thing.

The Badlands end about fifteen miles away from the city center in a wall painted like a group of trees. The wall can't be destroyed, can't be scaled, and can't be tunneled under. Trust me, I've tried. The fact that some of the highest level NPCs hang out in The Badlands keeps me from venturing out there much. Occasionally, when I feel like slaughtering, I'll make my way to the perimeters of the city in search of trouble. For better or worse, trouble usually finds me before I can find it.

"Cat got your tongue?" I ask Frances.

With her hair pulled back into a ponytail, her face seems sharper, more defined, hardened. There is a slight redness to her cheeks; her blue life bar is about three quarters full, which means she took quite a beating back at the hotel.

"I wasn't expecting the Reapers to show up so soon," she finally says.

"Where to?" the cab driver asks. He resembles all the other drivers in the city – overweight, under-shaven, indifferently bathed, surly, garrulous.

"Devil's Alley," I say through gritted teeth.

"Take it easy, sport." He locks eyes with me in the rearview mirror. A stained rag hangs from the mirror, burnt at the edges. My hand goes up to access my inventory list, but Frances stops me.

"You should kill less," she says under her breath. "It serves no true purpose."

"Listen to the broad," the cabbie says on the tail end of a gnarly cough, "sounds like nuggets of wisdom if you ask me."

"No one asked you, Buttinsky. If I want any shit out of you I'll squeeze your head." What I wouldn't give to taser the shit out of this driver, taser him until his eyes exploded out of his bulging fly-head. I cover my indignation by asking, "You said something about a glitch back in the hotel. Care to enlighten me?"

Frances keeps her head trained on the back of the driver's seat.

"Well? And don't give me this *you can't handle the truth* nonsense. Give it to me straight, Frances, lay it on me."

"You've been in C.N. – I mean The Loop – so long that you've begun talking like the NPCs here," she says, avoiding my question.

"I'm just trying to get my head straight, sister." I tell her. "You show up, tell me I've been here for eight years or so and then all sorts of shit starts happening. You'd be fired up too if you were in my shoes."

"It's complex."

"Well, un-complex it for me then, start with the basics. As my mom used to say, *use your words.* Who are those Raper guys that attacked us back there?"

"*Reapers.*"

"Yeah, whatever – what about 'em?"

"They belong to a murder guild that enters the various worlds inside the Proxima Galaxy to track players who are affected by the glitch and can't log out; players like you. Once they find you, they kill you."

"And then I respawn. What's the point?"

"No, they kill you for reals. If they kill you here, your body in the dive tank at the digital coma facility in Cincinnati, Ohio dies too. They use illegal weapons that override the safeties in your visor to fry your brain.

I sideline what she has just said and return to the Reapers. "So, their weapons essentially create a brain aneurism?"

"No. An aneurism is a burst blood vessel. Their weapons trigger a low voltage, high amperage discharge right through the brain that literally fries it."

"Thanks – good to have that straight. But why, then? What's the point in killing us?"

"They have people working on the outside that have already prepped all your assets, digital and otherwise, which will transfer to their organization once you die. They've done this hundreds of times now. They're quite good at managing the paperwork."

"I hardly have anything back in the real world…" I say. At least I think this is true.

"Not true. As you know, you can't log out, which means you are stuck here in… The Loop. The Proxima Company has given substantial sums to the people who have been trapped by the glitch that prevents you from logging out. It was the same glitch that I—"

"So the glitch prevents me from logging out. What about my repetitive days? Why is every day the same?"

"The NVA Seed – neuronal visualization algorithmic seed – is responsible for the repetition."

"Really? I was wondering if it was that…"

"The other players that I've rescued didn't experience the same thing as you, the repetition. Each world is different, highly manipulated by the NVA Seeds that oversee them."

"I've long since given up the search for the seed," I say, watching the city whiz by in a flurry of filth outside the taxi's windows. "Any clues on where I can find it?"

"I don't know," she says. "I haven't got that far yet."

The sound of a passing transport vehicle momentarily fills the interior of the taxi. Our driver slows down, letting the vehicle pass.

"Back to the Reapers – they're after money given to me by the Proxima Company due to the fact I'm stuck in The Loop, correct?"

"Exactly. They kill people and the money is transferred and shared among the members of their guild."

"But that's murder… "

"Legally it isn't. They've argued successfully in various jurisdictions that they are actually trying to free people, to help them log out of the various VE dreamworlds they're stuck in. They're quite good at what they do. There is *a lot* of money behind their organization now."

"They always win, don't they?"

"Who?"

"The bad guys."

Frances sighs. "Almost always."

~*~

Our taxi lowers into Devil's Alley, which gives Basin City a run for its money. Toppled trash cans sit along the street playing host to digital rats with long scaly tails, buckteeth and beady red eyes. My hand is already coming up to access my inventory list when I see the rats – nothing like a little target practice to start the day.

"Later," Frances says, squeezing my wrist. I turn to her, still mesmerized by the blue indicator over her head. *A real person...*

"How did you know what I was going to do?"

"Call it a hunch."

I detect a sparkle behind her eyes, but I ignore it.

I'm out of our taxi before Frances so I can scan the immediate area. The streets are practically empty aside from a few NPC fiends sitting in darkened corners with their knees to their chests, huffing Riotous from beer can pipes.

"We're good," I tell Frances.

She laughs as she steps out. "My hero."

The driver's window rolls down. "Are you going to pay me or not?" he asks. "I didn't drive all the way here for nothing."

The urge to bash him in the face with a golf club – item 333 – swells inside me. Frances pays him before I can react.

"Thanks for the tip, toots," he says as his window goes up. Air compresses and his jalopy shakes, lifting off the ground.

"Remember," she says, 'violence will only get you so far in The Loop. This is something you may have forgotten."

"Violence is The Loop and The Loop is violence. That's been my motto for as long as I can remember. Why would I change it now?"

"Why would anyone change anything?" she asks.

"Is that supposed to be some type of philosophical statement?"

"It's more of an observation. Come on, let's get to Barfly's."

A tin can hurls over my shoulder, slamming into a trashcan. I spin around to find dozens of bottles and cans hovering in the air.

"Is The Loop trying to kill us or something?" I ask.

"Something like that."

More cans zip through the air towards Frances. Her body shield protects her, flashes a green grid as the cans ricochet off her frame.

"Don't worry about the cans; they can't hurt us with our body shields on."

She turns into an alley and I follow, bottles and cans pelting us along the way. Occasionally the sound of shattering glass meets my ears, as some of the bottles are made of thinner glass than others. We advance towards Barfly's, moving in front of a few transients.

"Hey buddy... " one of the vagrants calls out. He's an ugly man with a blackened throat; a large bruise covering his left eye reminds me of Mount Fuji.

"What is it?" I ask.

"Can you spare some cred?"

"Why did the Proxima designers put so many fiends in this world?" I ask Frances. Before she can stop me, I retrieve a Glock 22, item 199, from my inventory list and paint the wall crimson with the back of the bum's head. The others quickly scatter.

"Quantum!"

"What?"

"You don't have to kill everything, you know."

"How would you have handled it?"

"I would have transferred him some money."

"Tried that before. I don't know how many times I have to tell you this, but violence is the answer to the enigma that is The Loop. Remember – I've been here a lot longer than you."

She huffs, "Keep your cool, got it?"

"The next thing you're going to say is that NPCs are people too."

"They *were* people… "

"What?"

Frances shakes her head. "Never mind."

"No, tell me."

"The majority of NPCs, aside from certain assassins, were once beta testers for the various Proxima Worlds, before the galaxy expanded. The Proxima Galaxy, which was based on primitive algorithms used in a game called *No Man's Sky,* randomly generates worlds, which are seeded – called niche seeding – and then *opened for population.* Think of the generation process as a sine curve, one simple equation known as the Superformula populates the Proxima Galaxy with various worlds, niche worlds marketed towards certain audiences. So there are dragon worlds, mining worlds, housewife worlds, high fantasy worlds, arctic worlds... you get the picture. Within these worlds, you can "play" the game by fighting, or going on quests. You can also simply exist, living your life within the world."

"So where do NPCs fit in all this?"

"You've forgotten everything..."

"Selective memory, I suppose."

Frances says, "At the start, before you or I started playing, regular players worked in-game jobs which allowed them to participate freely in various Proxima Worlds. Some were taxi drivers; others were bartenders or doormen at hotels. The Proxima designers captured all these interactions and expanded upon them using the Superformula, which strangely enough, was actually created in 2003 by a Belgium plant geneticist named Johan Gielis to study flora and predict its spreading patterns. You should already know all this, Quantum. NPCs *were* people too."

"But they aren't now."

"True, but they were, at some point. Anyway, you should be nicer to them. There is no telling what they may be able to tell you or help you with."

A neon sign flickers at the end of the alley. *Barfly's.* Gone are the NPCS hovering about, offering assassinations or quickies for a small fee. Gone are the candy men in baggy slacks hawking Riotous. The place would look somewhat cheerful if it weren't for the dried piles of vomit, the coagulating puddles of blood, the broken bottles and the syringes scattered around the entrance.

65

"Shall we?" Frances asks. A flying bottle hits her shoulder, deflected by her body shield. "There will probably be fewer bottles hurled at us inside."

I laugh. "You haven't spent enough time at Barfly's."

~*~

Croc the doorman pats me down, rougher than I would have liked.

"You know that won't help any, right?"

"Rules is rules, Quantum."

"When did you start patting people down? Hell, this is Barfly's, the Mos Eisley Cantina of The Loop. There isn't a better place to get stabbed in the back in the entire city."

"Watch it, Quantum." Good ol' Croc with his chiseled features, gargantuan size and fists the size of computer monitors. I've taken a good beating by those hands before. Claiming that the man packs a mean knuckle-sandwich is an understatement.

"The bar has disabled access to our inventory lists," Frances says under her breath.

"They've done what? What the hell is happening in here?"

"The Loop," she says, using my word for it. "You can't access weapons in here now. Don't worry, my mutant hacks aren't as easily affected by the game's AI."

Croc finishes *TSAing* me and moves onto Frances, who is more or less indifferent to the entire affair. I still haven't figured this little lady out. Sure, she's a tough cookie, but there's something she isn't telling me and I don't like it. This on top of the fact that she

66

has killed me twice is keeping me on my toes – there's no telling if she'll gut me again just for the hell of it.

"A seat at the bar," I say as I plop down in my favorite spot in the far corner. A glance around the gin mill I call a second home tells me something is off. Aside from a couple of generic NPCs playing pool in the back, the place is empty. Cid the bartender knows just what I want before I've even placed my tookus on the stool.

"Thanks for the beer, Cid."

"My pleasure. For the lady?" he asks slyly.

"A bottle of Jack, the biggest you got," she says.

"Coming right up."

He hobbles to the other end of the bar to find the bottle. Cid's got the greaser look down; his hair has been combed so many times it has formed a permanent crease in his hairline.

"A bottle of Jack? I didn't know you were that kind of lady."

"I'm not. You'll need a weapon if we're attacked while we are here. I figure a bottle of Jack will work."

Cid returns with a bottle and a single shot glass.

"Make it two."

"Bottles or shot glasses?" he asks.

"Shot glasses."

Moments later I'm pouring a shot for Frances.

"Let's make a toast," I say.

"To what?"

"To the damage we did to those Reaper goons back there."

She sets the shot I've just handed her on the bar and gives me a motherly look. "You really don't know what we're up against, do you?"

"Don't give me this shit, Frances. You keep up the mysterious act and parcel info out in baby *bytes*." I wince as the shot slides down my throat. The idea of alcohol is sometimes as powerful as the alcohol itself. My hand wraps around Jack's neck and I squeeze another shot out.

"You've become an animal in here," she says, watching me throw the shot back.

"You'd become an animal too if you were trapped in here for nearly two years."

"It's been nearly eight," she reminds me. "You seem to be suffering from a form of virtual amnesia."

"According to you!"

"And your calendar."

"Just... just... " Instead of arguing with her I pour another shot. Damn it feels good to pretend I'm becoming intoxicated.

"Relax, Quantum."

"You still haven't told me why you're here," I say.

"I'm here to help you."

"Help me what?"

"Get out of The Loop."

"What if… " I pause, weighing what I'm about to say next. Screw it, let the words flow. "What if I don't want out of The Loop? What if I like it here?"

"Well if you like it here, I can go now." She stands.

"Wait!" I look down at my fingers, which are now wrapped around her arm. "Sorry."

"It's fine."

Frances sits, brushes off the front of her tight black pants. She's a hotbody, but I have more on my mind than sex. Strange to say, but there are more important things in life.

"Take another shot," I tell her.

"Okay."

She opens the bottle and takes a swig.

"That's my girl!"

Frances smiles at me again. There's something about her smile that I recognize, something that reminds me of the real world. Two flashes come to me. In one, I'm kneeling in front of a girl who looks like a younger version of Frances. In the other, I'm settling into a large vat of liquid wearing a NV Visor.

"What is it?" she asks.

The concern on my face must be evident. "Who are you?" I ask, knowing that it's sometimes better to ask than answer.

"Frances Euphoria. And you?"

"Quantum Hughes," I say. "Wait, why are we telling each other our names."

"You asked first."

"But *who* are you? Why are you here?"

"I keep telling you, Quantum, I'm here to help you."

~*~

But what if I don't need help? What if I am secretly afraid to leave The Loop, afraid to see what has happened to my body in the real world? I must be puny by now, a small fry. In my calculations it has been two years. In Frances' (and for some reason the current in-game calendar) it's been eight. Either way, I'm likely a shell of my former self by now, a husk, a whisper, a wraith. Not that I was every jacked up or anything, but two to eight years in a digital coma has to have taken its toll. My Loop-life may not be half-bad to what I'll face on the outside.

As Frances speaks, I glance down at my hand, noticing the way the blond hairs are arranged in swirls near my wrists. My eyes move to my fingers, to my groomed nails, which never seem to grow in The Loop. Who is cutting my nails in the real world? Who is taking care of my body? Am I really in a dive vat in a digital coma unit in The People's Republic of Ohio? Of course I am, but who then has been looking after me for so long? *A nurse, you idiot,* I think, and to please this pessimistic voice, I take a long drag from the bottle of Jack.

"…that's why we need to get to The Badlands, to search for this logout point."

"Wait, there's a logout point in The Badlands?" I ask. "But that place is Nowheresville… "

70

"Yes, that's what I've been saying for the last few minutes. Haven't you been listening?"

"Sorry, I was thinking about something."

Cid stops by. "Wow, you two sure know how to put a bottle back. Would you like another?"

"Not now, Cid," I say. "We're busy."

"No problem, Quantum, just checking."

"You can go now," I growl.

He scuttles away and Frances shakes her head at me. "You really know how to treat people here in The Loop, don't you?"

"They aren't people."

"We can debate that later. We need to get to The Badlands… "

"But The Badlands are vast, I mean, they are much larger than the city. Hell, they surround the city. I bet they account for at least fifty percent of The Loops playable area."

"Sixty-two percent. This is why we should start searching now, before more Reapers come. We must find the logout point. It is the only way out."

"Why is there a logout point anyway? You said I'm stuck because of a glitch, right? Give me the lowdown; start from the top."

"The designers put a manual logout point in each Proxima World, just in case *they* got stuck during the creation process. They did this while they were developing the dreamscape, while they were still tweaking the neuronal algorithmic core. Remember, Proxima Worlds were designed from the inside out. That is, before the virtual big bang."

"Virtual big bang?"

"After the initial worlds were created, the Proxima Galaxy began spawning other worlds and caretakers – NVA Seeds – for these worlds, essentially a combination of entropy and dream-structuring through procedural generation. A virtual big bang, if you will. Every world created has the ability to create another world. People can buy these and turn them into whatever they'd like."

"Right."

"In the real world, you are here," she points to her forehead. "The prefrontal cortex, the home of your ego. Your pleasure centers are in the middle of your brain and your consciousness is behind your eyes, the orbital frontal cortex. When you dream, these things basically shut down, leaving us with the amygdala, which is when the neuronal visualization algorithm kicks in, activated by sensors on the NVA Visor you're wearing in the real world."

Another sip from the bottle and I tune back in to Frances.

"With your orbital frontal cortex knocked out, you can basically do anything in a dreamscape. This is why the Proxima designers created the advanced abilities bar, to limit what you can and can't do and how long you can do them for. Different worlds call for different advanced abilities and different sizes of these bars. The bars in epic fantasy worlds are longer. C.N. – I mean The Loop – is supposed to be gritty, supposed to be slightly surreal yet modeled off real life. This is why mutant hacks are banned here."

"You said that the designers created manual logout points in various Proxima Worlds."

"Yes, they did or the NVA Seed, the world's caretaker, did."

"Why didn't they release the locations? That would have made sense."

"There is a master list, actually."

"Well who has it?" I ask her. "Shouldn't we just ask them?"

Her eyes grow serious. "The Reapers have it."

"How did they get it?"

"By killing all the original Proxima Galaxy designers."

"In real life or in the Proxima Galaxy?"

Frances shrugs. "No one knows for sure. Both probably."

"So why don't we just capture one of the Reapers and give 'em the third degree?"

"As distasteful as I find it, we've actually tried that, and it never works – they always just log out. Anyway, only a few of the higher ups in the organization have access to the list."

"Well, we could bait the higher ups?"

"We should probably try and just find the logout point ourselves. I've been able to do it before, in a different Proxima World."

"What kind?"

"It was a dinosaur themed one called *Jurassic Virtual*."

"Whoa, did you ever fight a T-Rex?"

"No, but I rode a stegosaurus."

"That's the second coolest thing I've heard in two years."

"Eight years."

"Two years."

"How many days according to you?" she asks.

"Five hundred and forty nine days."

"That's just a little over a year and a half…"

I shrug. "Closer to two than I'd like."

~*~

Cid stops by, smiles at us through missing teeth. "Did I hear you two were going to The Badlands?"

"Shouldn't you be bartending?" I ask.

"No one to serve." He hunches over the bar. "What's this about The Badlands?"

"Nothing," Frances says for me. "We should be going, Quantum, before the bad guys show get the word on our whereabouts."

She squeezes my arm.

"Why would they get the word?" I get the drift and turn to Cid. "Say, you weren't going to drop a dime on us, were you?" My hands already on the bottle of Jack, ready to break it if need be.

"Easy, Quantum," he says, backing away.

Frances stands. "Let's go."

We're outside Barfly's before I can start any trouble. The sun has hidden like a coward behind a clump of sinister clouds, returning the ambience to Devil's Alley that I've grown accustomed to. I feel the urge to retrieve the Glock from my inventory list and shoot at the burning little beacon of false hope.

"Taxi?" I ask.

"The Badlands border Devil's Alley, do they not?"

"They border everything, from Chinatown to my favorite stomping grounds."

"We'll start there, in your... *favorite stomping grounds* as you say." A floating orb appears in front of Frances. She presses a button and the terrain of The Loop appears in a circular grid of light.

"That's pretty fancy."

"It's called an atlas sphere. This will make it easier for us to remember which portion of The Badlands we've already checked. Each portion we clear will appear red. This is us," she says, pointing at two blinking cursors. "I'm transferring you one now."

"I want to be green." An icon appears in front of me, indicating that item number 549 has been added to my inventory list.

"The user of the atlas sphere always appears green on the atlas. That's why yours is blue."

"Got it."

"Our atlas spheres are linked. Any information that appears on mine will appear on yours. Let's get started here." She presses her finger into the center of the projected map.

"From the small amount of data we have, it appears as if the logout point will be stationary."

"What does that mean?"

"It means that it could be anywhere, attached to anything. We'll have to clear the entire area."

"How long do you think that will take?"

"No telling."

Frances walks ahead of me past a pile of cans. Some of the cans lift into the air, smashing into her body shield.

"What's with The Loop anyway?" I ask as I swipe one of the cans out of the air. "Why is it attacking us all the sudden?"

"The Loop has basically gone into a defense mode. It feels…" Her eyes head north as she thinks of the right word. "It feels *threatened* by my appearance, by the fact you may be leaving soon."

"Threatened?"

A bottle smashes into Frances; the green grid of her shield lights up, protecting her body as she walks. "For some reason, the NVA Seed that monitors everything in The Loop *likes you*; it doesn't want you to leave."

"Likes… me?"

"Yes. I suppose *has an affinity for its only player* would be a better phrase, but you get the picture. The Seed likes that fact that you are here and it doesn't want to let go."

"So I have both Reapers and the world itself after me?" I chuckle at this thought. It's strange when something of pure science fiction lays such a heavy hand on a person's life.

~*~

A large rat appears in the window above the backseat of an abandoned car, eyes us curiously. I access my Beretta 92 with an ECO-9 silencer – item 501 – from my inventory list and fire a shot. I miss and the rat disappears.

Frances laughs and I fire one more shot at the gas tank. The explosion that follows is red, tipped in orange and white. A perfect explosion, like most of the explosions I've either witnessed or been killed by in The Loop.

"You sure are a tough guy," she says.

"That rat could have been spying on us… " I say.

"Actually," she turns to me, "you're right, it could have been."

I see the flicker of flames in the distance. The entrance to this part of The Badlands crosses over a drainage ditch filled with broken bottles. I was once tossed by an NPC down there – boy did it do a number on my back. I offed myself that day just so I didn't have to feel the injury any longer.

"There."

I point at a pair of boards that cross the moat of glass. The board on the left looks a little rotten, but my guess is that it's strong enough to support our weight, at least one at a time.

"What is it?"

Frances Euphoria hesitates. "I'm not a big fan of heights," she finally says.

"Even in a VE dreamworld?"

"Especially in a virtual entertainment dreamworld."

"Just use your advanced abilities."

There are two bars constantly visible in my field of vision. One is my life bar, which is blue. The other is my advanced abilities bar, green. I'm so used to seeing these things that I no longer notice them, unless they've been partially depleted.

"I'm sure you have enough juice," I say before launching myself over the ditch. I turn back to Frances. "You coming or not?"

"Actually, I'm still recovering from using my mutant hacks back at the hotel. That was quite the fight."

It's the first time I've seen fear on her face.

"Are you coming?" she asks.

I hurl myself back over the ditch, stopping directly in front of Frances Euphoria. We now stand intimately close, inches away from one another.

"Come on." I scoop her into my arms before she can protest and leap over the ditch.

"My hero," she says, rolling her eyes as I set her down. A taxi passes overhead, veering into a sharp U-turn. It continues back towards Devil's Alley looking for scum.

Directly to our left is an abandoned Ferris wheel, partially stuck in the ground. To our right is a funhouse, the entrance shaped like an evil clown opening its mouth. The clown's lips are blood red, its nostrils flared and its eyes white without pupils. With my Beretta still in my hand, I shoot out the clown's front teeth.

"I'm impressed," Frances Euphoria says in a way that tells me she isn't impressed.

An old transient, hunched over and carnie-like, limps towards us. The skin on his face is deformed, covered in pockmarks. A little top hat with a long peacock feather sticking out of its band sits on his head, tilted to the left. One arm is smaller than the other.

"Looking ... looking ... looking ..." he says frothing at the mouth. "Looking! Looking! ALWAYS looking ... I am ... you are ... we are ... ARGH! Knife me! LOOKING! Knife me! Blood like a hound keep your voices down ... keep them down KEEP THEM DOWN!"

"Stop right there, buddy," I say, aiming my Beretta at him. Frances lowers my arm.

"We're here searching for something," she says calmly.

His lips curl and his tongue darts over the tops of his teeth. "SEARCHING! Ha! Search we will 'til the earth ends and we begin and we begin and we begin ... " His eyes fill with tears. "WE BEGIN and we WE BEGIN begin and I ... and ... search and all the ... stationery HOLY EYES release I complete I forget ... forget ... FORGET!"

"I'm taking this one out," I say. "Something's wrong with him."

"Wait ... " Frances approaches the carnie. He shrinks into himself, the fat from his scarred cheeks flopping onto his shoulders. "Don't be afraid. I'm not going to hurt you."

He chatters, "Nothing to be afraid of NOTHING to be afraid ... to be ... scared feared reared seared cleared mirrored weird beard ... to BE ... or ... TO BE OR TO BE! Ah!" His beady eyes lock onto Frances. "AWAY!" he snarls. "Away! AWAY!"

I fire a shot directly over his head; the silencer muffles the report as the bullet cracks past. "ARGH!" He pulls on the brim of his hat as if he's trying to crawl inside.

"Quantum!"

"Leave this one alone, Frances. I'm telling you, I've been in The Loop long enough to know when something … "

The carnie leaps forward, sinking his teeth into her arm, somehow cutting through her body shield. She screams and her fist comes back, connecting with his eye. Once, twice. His eye bursts, spewing white acid into the air.

I'm already next to her by the time this happens, cracking the carnie in the back of the head with the butt of my Beretta. Still, he's unrelenting; he has practically super-glued his teeth into Frances' arm. I grab his feet, pulling at his ankles. His pants come down and shit trickles out of his ass.

"What in the … "

I grab the back of the carnie's head, pulling his body in a downward motion to avoid his digital shit. I'm too busy trying to avoid the crap misting out of his ass to see that Frances Euphoria's other arm has morphed into a hooked blade. She brings the blade down, amputating her own arm.

The carnie, now on all fours with his pants off and Frances' arm in his mouth, scurries off towards the funhouse. My finger goes up and my inventory list appears. A Molotov cocktail – item 51 – appears in my hand. I toss it at the clambering carnie and it explodes on impact.

"Sorry about your arm … "

I turn to find light spiraling around Frances' arm. The light is white on top, rainbow-colored on bottom, where it currently reforms her wrist.

"You can regenerate?"

"My avatar regenerates on her own," she says. "None of the weapons here can do much damage to me."

"What about the Reapers?"

"They have different weapons, ones that aren't available in this world."

"Come, let's keep exploring." Frances' atlas sphere floats in the air next to her. It begins zipping around, scanning areas with a red beam.

"Activate yours as well," she says. "It will make this much easier."

~*~

We search for hours after her arm has healed. Occasionally we encounter overly aggressive bums tweaked up on Riotous, but none as vicious as the strange carnie that attacked us earlier. According to Frances, nearly anything can be the logout point, as long as it is stationary.

The logout point must be stationary.

The sun sets (or at least it's the time that it should start setting – cloud coverage has made it nearly impossible to tell). At any rate, I've lived in The Loop long enough to know that night is a bad time to be in The Badlands. The number of hostile NPCs multiplies at night, which will make our search just that much harder. True, it doesn't really matter if I die or not, but every once in a while I like to actually make it through the day and go to sleep on my own. From what I can remember, the last day I lived through entirely was day 381, which coincides with the M-1 Garand that I picked up at The Pier. Nothing like eight rounds of .30-06 and a sixteen-inch bayonet to take out a few jobbies.

"We'd better take a powder," I suggest.

"Pardon?"

"Leave, we should leave."

"That's fine." Frances Euphoria's atlas sphere whirls around her head for a moment before materializing. "I need to log out anyway, eat some dinner. It's been a long day."

An incomprehensible sense of longing balloons within me.

"What?" she asks, noticing the half-frown on my face.

"Log out. I can't imagine what it would be like to actually log out, or to eat actual food for that matter. Do you … " I eye her wearily. "Do you know what has happened to me back in the real world? Have you … seen me?"

"I have, Quantum." She takes a step closer to me. "I see you every day."

"Really?"

A flare gun appears in Frances' hand, which is helpful for flagging down taxis in remote areas. She fires a round and within seconds, a taxi lowers itself to the ground.

"Where you heading?" the cabbie asks through the crack in his window.

"Mondegreen Hotel," I say.

"I wasn't going in that direction, but I guess I'll take you there."

I open the back door and slide in. "Well, excuse the Hell out of me for asking you to do your job," I say under my breath.

"A wise guy, eh?" His dark eyes size me up through the rearview mirror.

"Why don't you goose it and mind your own damn business."

"Quantum," Frances whispers as she scoots in next to me, "Manners."

"I hear you there, lady," the cabbie says as his taxi lifts into the air. "Kids these days get a kick out of being punks. Kind of shows you where the world is going."

"What was that?" I ask.

"Cool it, Quantum."

~*~

The Mondegreen Hotel is a somber affair, a grungy place with a chipped exterior and a few broken windows on the lower floors. Not exactly the Trump Taj Mahal.

The hotel has six stories if you don't count the basement, which used to be a bar. The entrance to the dreary hotel is marked by a few steps and a couple of dead bushes chock full of paper bags used to hold forties, condom wrappers, discarded weapons (I found item 266 in those very bushes – a burlap sack full of door knobs) and the occasional body part.

"Home sweet home," I say as the taxi lowers itself to the street.

I wanted to speak to Frances about my body in the real world, but I had decided to keep my mouth shut during the ride back to the hotel. The cabbie could have overhead us, which wouldn't have mattered to me in the past. Things have changed now that I know The Loop is trying to prevent me from logging out.

"Let's go to my room," I say as soon as the taxi lifts into the air. "Hey … "

"Yes?" Frances asks. Her hands are on her hips, parked just over her belt. There's something gorgeous about her, something overly familiar. I still can't place my finger on it.

"What did you mean when you said earlier that you saw my body every day?"

"I meant exactly what I said."

"What do I look like … in the real world?"

I've imagined what I look like countless times since being trapped here. There's no telling.

"Thin," she says, turning away from me. "You are very thin, Quantum, a shadow of your former self." A can lifts out of a trashcan and hurls itself at her. She brushes it away and it clinks onto the ground.

Her statement bothers me even though I've known for a while that this was likely the condition of my body in the real world. "You know, you haven't really told me *why* you are here to rescue me."

"It's a long story … "

"Yeah, you keep saying that too. Get on with it, doll face. Also, why do you see me every day? You stalking me or something?" I ask with a nervous grin on my face.

"Stalking? Hardly." Frances is facing me again, her red hair framing her face. "You really can't remember, can you?"

"Clue me in," I say. "I'm sick of being stuck in the dark here."

We enter the lobby of the hotel. The chandelier is half-lit as it always is, the carpets red and elaborate. The place is more or less spick and span; there's no evidence that we battled a load of Reapers in here for breakfast.

"Quantum ... " Frances stops dead in her tracks, her arms at her side with her palms open. My eyes fall upon a package on the receptionist's desk. "Run!"

Too late is an understatement.

The lobby walls last just long enough for the shockwave to splat us like roaches before they balloon outward ahead of the flame front. I never hear the façade of the hotel collapse into the street.

Day 550

Feedback like banshees entombed in my skull. Feedback, my Judas, my arch nemesis, my antagonist. My dreams are bitter tears, cries from the nucleus of a lost valley filled with murky characters and dagger-eyed snakes. I dreamt that I was in a vat of liquid being turned by a soft pair of hands. I dreamt that the hands moved up and down my body, massaging my nonexistent muscles. I dreamt of Frances and a time when she was younger, a time when we had reversed roles.

Loop dreams about a faux Loop-life while hoping to awake someplace else, someplace that isn't a digital cell, an algorithmic jail tied to an excruciating urge to awaken, to break myself free of the dream that I am prisoner to.

I can almost force myself awake in my dreams, almost separate myself from my avatar and travel upwards, towards the place we all must one day go. If only I could pry myself free of this body, peel my skin off and twist into the air, the wind trailing behind me as I spiral upwards towards a pair of eyes in the sky, my eyes in the real world, eyes that must be pressed before they can open in a different place.

A place that isn't The Loop.

I roll to my side wishing I were dead. My head aches, or at least I imagine it aching or at least it should be aching considering I've just woken after being killed by an explosion. I cast my qualms aside – Morning Assassin will be here any moment and I'd better be ready for him.

8:03 AM.

I scroll through my inventory list looking for the perfect way to defeat my opponent. He didn't come the previous morning, but that doesn't mean he isn't seconds away from breaking through my window ready to rumble. Feeling creative, I select a clothes iron which is always piping hot (item 93), and a trashcan lid (item 14), which makes a swell shield due to its thickness. My door springs open.

"There you are, you bastard!" I say waving my hot iron at … "Frances?"

"I thought I'd surprise you." She stands just beneath the door frame, wearing the same clothes she wore yesterday.

"Why didn't you just knock?"

"Why are you holding a trashcan lid and a clothes iron?"

"Because they won't hold themselves, Sugar Baby."

I press the button on the iron releasing a cloud of steam. The cloud quickly dissipates.

Frances' face twists into a disbelieving grin. "Quantum … you really have lost it in here, haven't you?"

"What?" I start laughing, and press the steam button again. "You should have knocked. I thought … I thought Morning Assassin was coming."

"Who?"

"My 8:05…"

"Oh, that's right. I keep forgetting you've been in here for eight years."

"Two years."

"Got it."

She walks over to my window, staring out at the city. I can see the slightest outline of her reflection in the glass.

"I have tons of questions," I say. Her visage morphs from light-hearted to serious. "First, regarding what we were talking about before we were blown to smithereens yesterday, I need you to be clear with me, Frances. I need you to be perfectly honest with me."

She turns to me. "Sit."

I relax back onto my bed.

"When one dives into a Proxima World, one does so unconsciously, essentially entering a prefab dreamworld that has been constructed using advanced neuronal algorithms."

"Which is why my real body is in what is known as a digital coma. I get it. Why are you telling me all this?" I ask.

"As I said yesterday, there are other people trapped in the various worlds of the Proxima Galaxy. And the Reapers hunt them down and kill them, for profit. Wherever the forces of evil attempt to extend their dominion, there is a counterforce that strives to oppose them. Just as SkyNet has John Connor, just as the Monarch has Brock Samson, the Reapers have *me!* I work for the FCG–"

"You're with the Feds?"

"Yes, I'm with the Federal Corporate Government." She clears her throat.

"I don't see you as a back-office bureaucrat, somehow."

"I'm part of a special division that locates and frees users who've been trapped inside Proxima Worlds."

"The FCG has a division for that? Who'd a thunk it?"

"They set it up in 2048 and you're one of the founders."

"Me?"

"You and one other guy ... "

"Tell it to the Marines, sister."

"Huh? What Marines? Wait. Ummmm ... I'm not kidding, Quantum. You're one of the founders and the first member of the team to successfully affect a rescue, back in 2050. There have been about a thousand other rescues since, but you were the first one to successfully go in, find a stranded user, locate the manual logout point, and bring them back."

"And I got stuck?"

"And you got stuck because of the glitch."

"And you're here to rescue me?"

"Bingo."

"Why did it take you so long to find me?"

"There is no way to tell which Proxima World a person is stuck in and there are tens of thousands of worlds – new worlds are created daily, as the Proxima Galaxy expands. As soon as someone loses the ability to log out, the system erases their data. I've been searching for you for the last four years. In fact, searching for you allowed me to save a few others."

"So people are still getting trapped?"

"No, not anymore. They eradicated the glitch 2055, after a massive overhaul of the code. However, there are still people trapped from before the glitch was fixed."

"How many?"

"Over a hundred."

"What about my partner, the other founder of this task force that searches for trapped players? What happened to–"

"–He's no longer with us," she says shortly.

"Okay, well what's the name of the task force anyway?"

"The Dream Team."

I snort through my nose at that.

"It used to be called the Dream Task Force, but people started referring to us as the Dream Team after the president gave a speech about us. Besides, the word *dream* is actually an acronym. It stands for *Dream Recovery Extraction and Management*. Most people just call us the Dream Team, though."

"Seriously? Wow! On a scale of one through ten on the Acme Relative Lameness Index, that's like an eleven. What wet end came up with that?"

"That *wet end* would be you, Mr. Hughes."

"Well, that explains some. I can be ironic at times." I smile at Frances but it seems to have no effect. "So what happens if I log out?"

"That's really up to you."

"And the bomb at the desk last night? Who planted that?"

"It was randomly generated. As I said earlier, the NVA Seed isn't happy."

~*~

I lead Frances downstairs (no assassins) and into the dining area. I figure a day of searching for a hidden logout point will require a big breakfast.

"Wait here a moment," I say after she sits. I whisk past Dolly, who is in the process of bringing us menus. I'm still kicking myself for killing her a couple days back – I feel guilty even though it had to be done, even though she came at me first.

"I'll be back in a moment, Doll," I say as I slip into the kitchen.

I kick the revolving door open and step in. A large meat cleaver zips past my face and lodges in the wall inches away from my shoulder.

"There you are!" I say to the chef with a grin on my face.

"Quantum!" I hear Frances call out from the dining room.

"Busy!" I yell back. My inventory list appears and I select a golf club – item 333 – and my metal trashcan lid (item 14).

The chef, a blubbery man with a handlebar mustache and a white chef's hat laughs. "Ha! You come at me with this?" he asks. "Pathetic!"

"It's been a few days you bastard," I say, baring my teeth.

He thrusts at me with an oversized carving knife. I deflect his attack with my shield and I nail him in the nuts with my nine-iron.

"OOooOOF!" His eyes bulge, his dentures fly out of his mouth, skip across the utility island and land in the Fry-O-Lator – I do believe I'll pass on the fries today. His face

91

purples as he bends forward, clutches his groin, and falls face-first into the salad prep station.

"I got you now, foul filet defiler," I shout, the bloodlust upon me.

"Sez you!" He whirls and flings a handful of chopped onion in my eyes, follows it with a sweet left hook – right cross combo. I back-pedal across the greasy floor, lose my footing and land flat on my back. The golf club flies from my grip and the trash can lid clangs away out of reach. A sack of flour hits me in the face, followed by a canister of sugar, a flat of eggs, and a gallon jug of cow juice. I hope there's enough left for pancakes when I'm done in here.

The kitchen door swings open. Frances Euphoria points her own .500 magnum at the chef. "Don't move and nobody gets hurt," she advises him. He slams on the brakes and freezes in place, an extra-large rolling pin cocked over his shoulder like a Louisville Slugger. With a roll of her eyes and an exasperated sigh she queries, "Seriously Quantum? This is something you *had* to do? You can't just leave him alone?"

"He's my ... " I look at my nonexistent watch. "Well, he used to be my 8:23 but I'm a little early. I thought maybe you'd like an uninterrupted breakfast."

The door swings closed and Mr. Chef leaps for me. I roll out of his way and he face-plants in the impromptu pancake batter.

I access my inventory list before he can reorient himself and come after me again. A dart gun – item 78 – appears in my hand. I fire a poison dart right into his neck; his hand flies to the dart as toxic yellow foam boils out of his nose and mouth. He twitches his faux life away and makes a pancake batter angel on the tiles as he does so.

I pick up the chef's rolling pin and add it to my inventory, item 550.

92

~*~

"Really, Quantum," Frances Euphoria says after I've returned to the dining area. "You are like a man-child in here, like ... like ... like an ape gone ape."

"Relaxitrate, Frances, I was just having a little fun. Besides, that chef has tried to kill me ... well I don't know how many times." I think for a moment. "At least a hundred times, at least."

"What'll it be?" Dolly appears with the menus in her hands and a pained expression on her face.

"Hiya Dolly," I say with a nervous grin. "Sorry about the other day ..."

"Which other day?" she asks, cocking her head to the right. "What would you like to eat this morning?"

Really? Nothing.

"I'll have the usual."

"Eggs over easy, three pieces of toast, bacon and a beer?"

"Add some pancakes too. Three, no make it four, extra butter."

There's something different about Dolly's makeup today. It's more elaborate than usual, especially around her eyes. Her lips aren't blood red as they normally are; instead they're pink, a faint color closer to orange sherbet than pink in the traditional sense. Her apron is different and reveals more cleavage.

"Will there be anything else, Mr. Hughes?"

Mr. Hughes? She's never called me that before. I put the pieces together, glancing from Dolly to Frances.

"She's just a friend," I say, nodding at Frances.

Dolly's cheeks redden. "What would you like, Quantum's friend?"

"I'll have a cup of tea," she says. "No, you know what, make that a beer."

"Two beers and the usual," Dolly says without making eye contact with either of us. She swivels on her heels and glides away.

"What was that about?" Frances asks.

"Well … "

"Well what?"

I say, "We are sort of a thing."

"Sort of a thing?"

"You know, jacketed, going steady."

"You're dating an NPC?" Frances presses her hand over her mouth to stifle a laugh.

"What's wrong with that? I've been here for nearly two years!"

"*Eight.* I just wasn't expecting that."

"What, you haven't encountered that before?"

"Actually, I've encountered it plenty of times. The lady trapped in *Jurassic Virtual* was having a relationship with a Velociraptor."

"How does that work?"

94

"About like you'd expect: scaly, with lots of scratching and clawing and biting – and that was just her."

"Sounds … uncomfortable."

"She did die a lot."

"Well, anyway, that's why Dolly was acting screwy. She's a little jealous."

"Strange," Frances says. "I've never seen an NPC look so … jealous."

"Dolly isn't like the others."

All the times we've shared come to me in a single image of us lying on my bed, each smoking cigarettes. Sure, we had sex, but most of the time we'd simply lie around until she had to go back to work or I felt like going on a hunting spree. Sometimes we'd break into the room next door and watch black and white detective flicks on TV, Dolly lying with her head on my stomach as she slept. Two (or eight) years are a long time to be with someone, even if that someone isn't actually a *someone.*

"She tried to kill me that night that I met you at Three Kings Park. That was the first time Dolly ever tried to do anything like that," I say. "It really got to me. I hated seeing her bleed, even though it wasn't real."

"Just because you're in what is essentially a programmed dreamworld, doesn't mean that emotions aren't real. If you experience it, it is real to you."

Dolly comes with the beers.

"How's work?" I ask her.

"I have to do all the cooking myself when you kill the chef," she says sharply. "You should remember that next time."

My mouth drops open. In all the times I've sent the chef to sit at the feet of Julia Child, Dolly has never once acknowledged my actions.

~*~

I wave at Jim the Doorman as Frances and I exit through the lobby. He nods at me nervously, avoiding eye contact.

"Cat got your tongue, Jim?"

"No, Mr. Hughes."

"Please, Quantum. Call me Quantum."

"No, Mr. Quantum."

"No messages?"

"None that I'm aware of, sir."

Frances smiles at Jim. "Have a nice day," she says, hooking her arm through mine.

"Thank you," he says in resonant, round tones. "I will certainly try."

The hotel doors swivel open and I step out, taking in what's left of the morning rays. Like yesterday, the rain clouds that have plagued my life since the start of my entrapment are nonexistent. The sky is tinted gray, but this could be a pollute haze as much as it could be an indication that rain would soon come. Still, the sun is evident.

"Where to, Ms. Euphoria? Or is it Mrs.?"

"Miss," she says.

Her atlas sphere appears in the air and a map of the city stretches in front of us, bathed in light. A small section of The Badlands near Devil's Alley is now colored red.

"That's the area we cleared yesterday," she reminds me.

One look at the map reminds me of how long this little mission is going to take. I don't know what the area of The Badlands corresponds to in miles, but it is expansive.

"Is there any place that would be better to check than others?" I ask. "I mean, are there any telltale signs of a logout point?

"Not to my knowledge. The manual logout points are randomly generated and then set in stone, wherever they may be. As I said earlier, a list exists, but the Reapers have it and they're not telling."

"Well if that's the case, we could check the area of The Badlands that borders The Pier. I haven't seen the water illuminated by the sun in … I don't know how long."

"Good. The Pier it is." Frances raises her hand and a taxi lowers itself to the ground. "Be nice to the driver," she says as we get in.

~*~

The Pier and its surrounding docks are modeled after New York Harbor sans the Statue of Liberty. The Badlands start just after a long series of warehouses, which are filled with everything from assassin lairs to massage parlors to drug manufacturers. I suppose everyone needs to get their jollies.

"Do you feel like busting a few Riotous manufacturers while we're here?" I ask after I've paid the taxi driver. His cab putters into the air, coughing up exhaust fumes.

97

"That's not really why we're here."

I shrug. The reflection off the water is indeed beautiful, even with the gray sky. "I was into the stuff about a year ago, during one of my ..." I bite my bottom lip. "During one of my darker spells. Riotous made me über-violent."

"I can't imagine you more violent than you already are."

Frances scoops her red hair off her forehead, pulls it back into a ponytail. The stink of The Badlands has a way of jolting me awake like a cup of strong Joe. The grime covered streets and the dead carcasses of a few choice varmints make me miss the comforts of my yellowed hotel room back at the Mondegreen Hotel. A couple of bums lurking behind a large dumpster remind me to keep my guard up. Home is where the grime isn't.

"What can I say? I'm a product of my environment."

Her atlas sphere appears in the air. "Shall we get started?"

"The Badlands border the warehouse area, across from the docks," I tell her with a sweeping gesture. "At night, there's a black market through one of the alleys. It's a swell place to find just about anything, from Riotous to weapons."

The sphere burns off and Frances follows it.

Watching her move and seeing the blue indicator above her head never ceases to amaze me. Having not seen a real, live person in at least two years, maybe longer, has made little things such as a player indicator much more fascinating than they should be. As we look for the logout point, I get to thinking about my age. According to myself, I'm in my thirties, thirty-three to be exact. *But if I've really been in here for eight years ...*

"How old am I?" I ask her. "In the real world ... "

"Close to forty. What's wrong?" she asks after noticing the frown on my face. "Trust me, you don't look a day over thirty in the real world ... pale, but a pale thirty."

"I just thought that I was thirty-three. I should be at day 550 or so. Keeping track was the one thing I managed to do right every day."

"The reason your days are off from the days that have passed in the real world is due to your sleeping habits, or more appropriately, your respawning habits."

"My sleeping habits?"

"You sleep longer now when you wait to respawn, or when you are killed. What was once more or less equivalent to the time passing in the real world has now ballooned."

"Ballooned to what?"

"It varies, but you can be asleep in the real world for up to ten days, sometimes thirteen."

The sound of a tugboat coming into The Pier pricks my ears. I've seen dozens of boats in The Pier, but they haven't moved in to dock until now.

"Frances," I say as the tugboat pulls in.

Water sloshes against the side of the boat, painting wet bands against a bow covered in orange rust. Thunder clouds bubble in the sky above, as if the AI running the place knows something bad is about to happen.

"Yes?"

"Is there something ... off about that boat?"

"What do you mean?" she asks.

My inventory list appears in front of me and I choose a pair of Leaks, item 16. They're handy for both infrared work and long distance viewing. The Leaks appear on my face in the form of steampunk-inspired goggles. My hand comes up to the left side of the Leaks and I adjust my viewing trajectory. "Well beside the fact I've never seen one come in to dock, I've also never seen one filled with people."

"Filled with people?"

The door on the wheelhouse spills open and bodies fall out, cracking their heads on the handrails. They're naked, zombie-like, with bleached skin covered in seeping whiplashes and reddened scabs. They continue spilling out of the door, crawling over one another, man and woman alike, clawing at each other with arrowhead-shaped fingernails as they gravitate towards the wharf.

Some of them hit the quay before I can access my inventory list. They fall on top of one another, crushing the others beneath them as they bark, growl, gnash their teeth, scream at the darkening sky.

A bazooka, item 82, appears in my hands in a matter of seconds. A targeting icon appears in the ocular feed provided by my Leaks. I lock onto the wheelhouse.

"Quantum ... "

"*What?*"

"Don't."

"Don't what?"

She hesitates as the bleached skin people pull themselves to their knees, fall over one another, bulge up the dock and onto the pavement separating The Badlands from The Pier. All of them have collars around their necks with blinking red lights.

"Frances, we've got a CHUD fest bearing down on us and you want me to hold fire."

My finger touches the trigger, ready to pull it.

"They're not NPCs." she says. "They're human."

~*~

"Human!? There must be hundreds of them!"

The bleached folk close the distance between us, coming on like rabid rats as they scramble towards us.

"These are people that have been imprisoned by Reapers," Frances explains quickly. "The Reapers send them to various Proxima Worlds to hunt for key players, players who have received money from the company, players like you. They're kept in solitary confinement until they are unleashed onto a dreamscape. If they successfully capture someone, they're supposedly freed and allowed to return to the real world. *But they are never actually released.*"

I turn back to the bleached people, watching them move closer. I can see their red eyes now; many of them suffer from some type of skin pigment disease. Portions of their bodies are milk chocolate brown, other parts are pig pink and rimmed with age spots. All but a few are completely nude.

"Can I kill them?" I ask.

"No, it's illegal. We could be charged with murder!"

"By *who,* exactly? We got freakin' zombies closing in on us and you're worried about legal niceties? What, the Society for the Prevention of Cruelty to Zombies is gonna come 'round and slap the bracelets on us? Hello, Frances – we have to be *not dead* here for that to happen!"

"Those collars around their necks prevent them from logging out and trigger a violent epileptic seizure if another player kills them. If their collars are damaged here or in any Proxima world, they'll die in the real world, and various RevCo shell companies collect their insurance payouts."

"So if I kill them I'm doing the Reapers a favor?"

"Plus, you could be charged with murder."

"Yeah, you said that, but only if I wake up."

" … but only if you wake up."

"I'll take my chances."

To one knee I go, aiming my bazooka towards the center of the moving mass of people, where it will do the most damage. "What are you waiting for, Frances? There's no time to kill like the present."

She steps in front of the muzzle of the bazooka, presses it into her stomach. "It's murder … "

"Move! They're getting closer."

"Put your weapon away, I'll … I'll handle this."

A metallic sphere spins in the air. Digital rain spews out of the bottom of the sphere, covering us with a blue dome of light that's been threaded together like a chain-link fence.

"Is it a one-way shield?" I ask. "Out but not in?"

"Yes."

"Good." I quickly access my inventory list and find my mini-gun, item 198. I should be able to mow 'em down like weeds with that.

"Quantum … "

"What's the problem, Boutros? Just in case your little diplomatic mission doesn't work."

It doesn't take long for the bleached people to reach the dome that surrounds us. They hurl themselves at it, scream and snap their jaws. Each time they touch the shield they're zapped by a jolt of electricity, which only infuriates them even more. Frances waits long enough for the people to realize they can't get to us before saying, "Who is your leader?"

A woman with clumps of hair sticking out of her head and lips ringed with blood hisses, "We have no leader…"

"Ah, so you're the leader," Frances says.

"She's not the leader." A man wrinkled like a hairless cat steps forward. He grabs the woman by the throat and she swings her fists into his face, smashing his teeth and bloodying her knuckles.

"These people are animals … "

"Some of them have been held prisoner for six years," Frances says under her breath. If you fire on them, you may hit their collars, so stay frosty." She turns to them. "You've come here to hun t... " She points at me. "Quantum Hughes, yes?"

The bleached people began squealing, spitting, screaming, seething and everything in between.

"Nice going, kid."

"You could help us instead," Frances suggests. "If we can find a logout point, we'll be able to log out and rescue you."

"Rescue us?"

Whispers spread through the crowd. Lightning cracks in the sky above, signaling that the normally dreary day of The Loop is making a comeback.

"Lower the shield and we'll do as you ask," the bloody-knuckled woman says.

Another man, his chin and neck covered in dried blood laughs maniacally. He grabs the woman by the back of the head and pulls her into the crowd.

"They're animals ... " I whisper. My hand drops to Frances' shoulder. "We'd be doing them a favor by ... killing them. You don't have to – I'll do it myself."

"No," she says, "we must try."

The crowd of bleached people stops swarming. The woman's body lifts into the air, covered in bite marks and scratches. Her lower intestines are pulled out of her body only to be chewed by a pair of twin girls. The man with blood dripping down his chin holds one of her eyeballs. He examines the shiny hunk of flesh before tossing it into his mouth, chewing it as if it were a grape. Still, no one touches the collar on her neck.

My inventory list appears in front of me.

Regardless of what Frances thinks, I know better than to let our shield down to these monstrous creatures. They've long since lost anything they have in common with humanity. I select a jacket lined with explosives that is triggered by the touch of a button on the sleeve (item 300). Sometimes suicide bombing is the best way to clear a whole slew of NPCs in The Loop. My guess is it will apply to the bleached people as well.

"I'm going to lower the shield," Frances is saying, her hands in front of her in a calming gesture.

"Good," the man with the bloody chin says. "We can make a deal if … if you treat with us as equals."

Another fight breaks out; the crowd swells and morphs as a few limbs and bloodied bits of flesh are tossed into the air.

"Frances," I say through gritted teeth, "Do not drop our shield."

"Quantum, you have to trust people," she says, "just as you've trusted me."

"But you're … "

"Human? So are they."

I glance through the blue chain-link barrier provided by our shield. I see a few faces at the bottom of the crowd, gnawing on the ankles of others and getting stepped on, stomped out. This is going to be bad.

"You said they'll hold us until the Reapers come, right?"

"Yes."

"The Reapers are already here."

105

~*~

A yellow portal appears in the sky, fizzing and spitting electricity. Four men wearing distended skull masks land on the ground. They're wearing the same stuff yesterday's losers wore – black leather studded with bones and teeth, armor, chains, spooky hoods and spiked boots. It's like S & M night at the *Pink Oboe*.

The bleached people pull back, visibly afraid of their captors. "They're here! They're here!" they point and shout.

The four Reapers walk through the line that the people have formed. One of the Reapers swings the butt of his weapon at a man with the body of a skeleton, knocking him to the ground. He roars as his hood comes off, revealing his bizarre skull mask. The Reaper brings the butt of the gun down onto the back of the bleached man's skull, crushing it like a watermelon.

"When can I shoot them?" I ask.

Frances' arm slowly morphs into a long, curved blade with a weapon on top, almost like a bayonet beneath a gun with a melon-sized barrel.

"I have to get me one of those … "

"You used to have one," she says, her eyes locked on the approaching Reapers.

"Will this shield protect against their blasts?"

"Not for long … "

"So what are our options here? Fight or flight?"

"Fight." she says, and the tone of her voice indicates to me that this isn't exactly how she'd like things to go down. "Avoid hitting the bleached people."

"I'll get right on that … "

One of the bleached men, the first one from earlier calls out to the Reapers. "I found them!" he cries. "Me! You should free me! I'm the one … "

Someone fists him in the back of the neck and spurs the inevitable brawl. The bleached people beat and chomp at each other but still keep their distance from the Reapers.

"Enough!" The most aggressive Reaper unloads a round into the air and the bleached people scatter.

"They have the right idea," I say.

"Now!" Frances points her weapon at the Reapers. A bright green blast spirals out of the barrel of her gun-arm, tearing through the man. My mini-gun spins up and hoses out a river of supersonic metal. The remaining three return fire and the shield drops.

I use the mini gun like a garden hose, but the Reapers don't seem to notice. I burn through more than half my ammo before I look down to find something clamped onto my leg. Three bleached people look up at me, their mouths filled with saliva as they bare their yellowed teeth.

More crawl in my direction.

"Don't kill them!"

"Dammit Frances!" I say as I kick my feet.

She blasts another Reaper in the chest with her gun-arm. It tears through his armor; digital blood sprays out of the back of his body. *Two Reapers down, two to go.* I have my own problems – the bleached people are up to my waist now, clawing me with their nails and sinking their teeth into my avatar.

I activate my advanced abilities and leap – slow motion – walking on air towards the two Reapers left standing who are now moving at a snail's pace. Suddenly, my advanced abilities bar disappears and I'm left kicking and twitching as I fall to the ground, directly on top of one of the Reapers that Frances has already smoked with her mutant hack.

My hand lands on his distended skull mask and I grip it tightly, triggering the mini-gun and blasting what has always been, up until now, a copper-jacketed wall of death at the other Reapers who are tag-teaming Frances. Fired cases fly out of the ejection chute in a cloud of brass; the gun goes silent as the last round goes downrange. The electric motor still spins the barrels until I release the trigger.

Bleached people squirm all around me, covering my face with their hands and digging their razor nails into my flesh. Breathing heavily, salivating, biting into my flesh. An explosion erupts ten paces away. My eyes are open just long enough to see two Reaper skulls flying through the air alongside Frances Euphoria's gun-arm.

They've killed Frances!

The bleached people overwhelm me. They cover everything until I can barely open my mouth, like quicksand, like a pit of ravenous snakes, like a swimming pool full of leeches. There's only one thing I can do.

I trigger my explosive jacket and flash into painless, instantaneous dissolution.

Day 551

Feedback licks the inside of my skull. Feedback travels from ear to ear laying waste to what's left of my sanity. Feedback an anathema, a constant reminder of the place I remain trapped, imprisoned.

I roll to my side, directly onto a Reaper's skull mask.

"Strange … " I say, examining the mask.

The Loop is out to get me, to disorient me. I've never awakened with something in my bed before, yet here it is – a Reaper's skull mask, item 551. The jaw of the skull mask is crushed, providing just enough covering for my nose, my cheeks and my forehead. The electronics inside seem to be intact.

As soon as I place the mask on my face, an ocular feed activates, showing me the gridline architecture of my hotel. The mask allows me to see to the floor below, where I find the child on his bed. It also allows for me to see into the hallway, akin to the way that one would look at a 3-D model of something and be able to zoom through it, from one portion to the next.

"Long distance," I say, and the hotel room's wall appears in my feed, magnified to a gross extent. I smile and my cheeks scrape against the inside of the Reaper mask. I have become the enemy I never knew I had.

Frances should be here any moment; at least I hope she comes. She never said what would happen to her if a Reaper punched her ticket.

She can't be dead.

8:04 AM.

"Where are you Frances?" I say, as if speaking aloud has ever done any good in The Loop. Stepping out of bed, I quickly move to the mirror on my dresser to see what my new skull mask looks like.

Just like the Reapers, my pupils aren't visible in the mask. The top of the skull stops just below my widow's peak, giving space to my blondish-brown hair. Unlike a normal skull, there is actually a *bone* protecting my nose.

I'm just about to take off the mask when the window shatters and Morning Assassin rolls into the room.

"You're back!?"

A throwing star lodges in my chest and the curare starts to take hold. He tosses another, but I've already activated my advanced abilities, and am *bullet-timing* back out of its path.

My inventory screen comes up and Morning Assassin freezes. I locate my harpoon, item 236, and the list disappears. I gasp – he's no longer in the same place he'd been when I accessed my inventory list.

"That's not going to work anymore, Quantum."

He grabs a handful of my hair and yanks my head back, exposing my throat. An icy blade spears into the side of my neck, and even though I know better I jerk backwards to get away from it as he rips it forward and severs all my tubes and pipes. M.A. releases his grip and my knees won't support me. I fall to the floor in a pool of my own blood, and he looms above me, good ol' number 33 gripped in his fist.

As my vision goes from red to gray, I realize that I'm really, *really* starting to hate that knife!

Exit, stage left. Fade to black.

Day 552

Feedback, you shitmonger. Before awakening in the hard-boiled hell of all hells, I dreamt that I was being washed, that someone was caring for me, turning my body over, cleaning me, keeping me alive. Of course all this is shattered by the violent static of the feedback.

Of course I wake up in The Loop.

"Bastards … " I say as I roll to my side.

Morning Assassin will be here any moment and I want to make sure he gets some good ol' fashioned payback for cutting my throat the previous day. My inventory list comes up and I access my chainsaw – item 112. What better way to start the morning than by flinging flesh and slinging blood?

I lower myself onto my haunches next to the dresser and my eyes fixate on the picture of the sinking sailboat that rests over my bed. The swelling colors whip their hues into a sea of remorse and anger. Apropos to say the least.

The time appears in front of me – 8:05 AM. Morning Assassin will come through the window any moment now and I'll be here to greet him with a chainsaw in the gizzard. Pay it forward or pay it back – the chainsaw conundrum.

Patience, Quantum.

I tug the starter rope once; the engine fires and the chainsaw roars to life as I goose the throttle. I can feel the chainsaw vibrating in my hands, whirring and ready to devour limbs.

To kill is to be part of The Loop.

The window shatters and Morning Assassin rolls in. He bounces to his feet I am on him like poo on a pig. It's as if I'm wielding the Mother of All Chainsaws; in one fluid sweep, both legs come off at mid-thigh. Before Ol' Lady Gravity can fully embrace him in his newly altered state, I pivot through a full three hundred and sixty degrees and swing the bar up under one arm, over his head, and down through the other. He collapses to the floor like some simile that doesn't involve *strings* and *marionettes* and lies there like the main attraction in *Boxing Helena*.

The chainsaw throttles down to a loud idle; I breathe in the heady stink of burned forty-to-one. "Anything you'd like to say before I finish the job? Anything at all?"

Morning Assassin shoots me a twisted grin. "Right, I'll do you for that!" he giggles. The gun barrel emerges from the back of his throat as a vein pulsates on the side of his face.

"What, the ol' roscoe-in-the-piehole gag again?"

The saw screams up to a zillon RPM as I mash the trigger and jam the tip of the bar right in his mouth. I take his head off and quarter his torso, just to be sure.

I return the chainsaw to my inventory list and step over to the mirror. Blood and scraps of flesh are splattered all over my face and shirt and speckle the walls, floor, and ceiling of my ultra-deluxe accommodation. No doubt Leatherface, Jeffery Dahmer, and Doctor Crippen are all weeping tears of pride at my morning's work, but for me it's just another day at the office.

Movement in my peripheral vision; one of Morning Assassin's severed arms twitch, the hand contracts into an almost-fist and gives me the finger. I almost laugh. Almost.

A change of clothes. The blood disappears from my skin, a black suit with a black tie and black cufflinks appears on my body. I select the Reaper's skull mask from my inventory list, item 551, and slick my hair back. Just in case, I select my jacket lined with explosives, item 300. This fits conveniently over my suit jacket; it doesn't look half-bad either.

I raise my finger at my reflection, making a gun out of my pointer finger and my thumb.

"Blam."

The crow appears on the windowsill and I don't even need to look at the time. The dark clouds will follow and somewhere, The Loop's NVA Seed is laughing at me. No matter. In times of great distress, the ability to maim will suffice.

I step into the hallway and the lights flicker three times. That means that it's assassin time again, and that there'll be six of 'em in the lobby below. *Be prepared* I always say, and a crowbar of the finest titanium – item 141 – appears in my hand.

I clear my throat as I walk down the stairs to the lobby in an all-black suit and a skull mask. *Don't fear the reaper – see the reaper; be the reaper. Na-na-na-na-na-na-na-na-na.*

The lobby.

Sure enough, one of the assassins comes from the left. The pry end of the crowbar spears through his open mouth and out the back of his skull With slow-motion activated (for everyone else but me), I twist under the next assassin's dagger, and crunch the crowbar against the side of his neck. From there time speeds up, and I'm in the air above two more assassins, standing with one foot on each of their shoulders with my legs spread, grandstanding. I swing the crowbar like I'm Tiger Woods teeing off pre-Elin Nordegren, and I outen the lights on both of those mugs.

Number five gets the hook end in the stomach. When I flip him up and over, land him pile driver-style and snap his neck, I also inadvertently discover what a Scotsman wears under his kilt when it flops down under his arms – the kilt, I mean. I unhook him and sling the crowbar backhand into Tail End Charlie's face, do a fancy jump-roll-and-spring-to-my-feet, snatch the crowbar before it falls, pirouette and cave in his skull with it. I raise both arms in the air and bow to the imaginary panel of judges.

That's how you bump off six assassins in less than thirty seconds.

"Mi ... Mi ... Mister Hughes?"

My eyes lock on Jim the Doorman. The Reaper's skull mask I'm wearing provides extra data on NPCs, including their combat ability and likelihood for Randomly Generated Mutant Hacks. Jim's combat ability is low, but his RGMH likelihood is high, over fifty percent. I remember the fight we had just a few days ago and I decide to prevent the battle before it starts. A targeting icon appears in my ocular feed and I toss the crowbar at Jim, connecting the sharp end with his chest.

"Call me Quantum, dammit."

~*~

It's amazing how easy it is to get back into one's routine. After corpsing Jim with the crowbar, I head to the kitchen, where I walk in, pop the chef between the eyes with one round from item 501, a silenced Beretta 92, and exit before he hits the floor. From there I head to the main dining area, just in time for Dolly to sashay to my table.

"I'll have my usual, Dolly," I say.

"What's with the skull mask?" she asks, her brows furrowing. "Have you … "

"Have I what?"

"Nothing."

A quick glance at Dolly shows me that her combat level is a lot higher than Jim's, surprisingly higher, astronomically higher, with a 100% chance of a Randomly Generated Mutant Hack. I need to stay on my toes like a ballerina.

"What are you looking at?" she asks.

"Me? A good looking gal with legs up to *there* and a knock-out pair of sweater-fillers. Say, Dolly, want to catch a flick later?" I ask for old time's sake.

"I'm busy." A flush spreads across her cheek. "Besides, you'll probably be busy with that other dame."

"Which other dame?" I ask, just for sport.

"The one that was in here the other day." Dolly is smacking gum and the ends of her sentences are accented with an annoying popping sound. "You know, the one with red hair."

"Frances Euphoria."

"Yeah, her."

"Actually," I say, dropping the show. "Have you seen her? I'm kind of looking for her. Something … happened to us the other day."

"Haven't seen her."

"Would you tell me if you had?"

"No," she says with a flirty grin.

"Well then how do I know if you're lying or not?"

"I guess you don't."

"Well that ain't fair, is it Dolly?"

"Life ain't fair, Quantum."

"Why don't you sit down for a moment, let's talk this through. I want to be honest with you for once."

Dolly hesitates. Her hand falls to the chair.

"Take a load off," I tell her. "I want to tell you what's going on, who that lady was and why I'm wearing this mask. You must know something is up… "

"You can't leave," she says, her eyes filling with tears.

"Can't leave?"

"Never mind. What do you want? Your usual?" She sniffs, wipes her nose. "Pancakes?"

"Dolly, why are you crying?"

"Quantum, tell me what you want or… or get the hell out of the dining room."

"Well hell, Dolly, I'm not trying to upset you. I just wanted to be honest with you."

"And take that mask off … I … I hate it!"

"It's helpful. It gives me extra data on the environment, architectural gridlines, NPC stats. I could use it … " The thought comes to me. "When searching for a logout point."

117

"So you do want to log out, huh? It's true," she says. "I ... I knew it!"

"Of course I do, Dolly, I'm trapped. I'm ... I'm human!"

She crosses her arms over her chest. "Am I not enough for you?"

"What?"

"AM I NOT ENOUGH FOR YOU, QUANTUM!?" she yells in a voice that isn't hers. It sounds like a thousand voices, a million bees buzzing around in my skull. It sounds like my morning feedback amplified.

~*~

"I don't want breakfast."

I push my chair away from the table.

"Fine."

"Come on, you're not sore are you?" I ask Dolly.

"Go find your logout point, if that's what you want!" she says and with that she's gone, veering towards the kitchen. I think for a moment to go after her, but I decide to deal with her later, if I make it to later.

I step out of the hotel and hail a taxi. One appears moments later, its hood shiny from the falling rain. Lightning cracks in the sky like flash photography. I'm in the taxi before I can even remember where I'm going.

" ... I said, where to pal?"

I glance at the taxi driver through his rearview mirror. He's the same as all the others, a human fly covered in little hairs with big bloodshot eyes and cigarette burns on his wife beater. Chrome-dome bottom feeder. My eyes skip from the driver to the faded hula girl affixed to his dashboard.

"The Pier. Make it fast, buster."

"Yeah, yeah. Make it fast. Everybody's in a hurry … " he grumbles as he lifts into the air. Just seeing the expansive city light up below us, and the rain lash against the windshield, makes me want to go for a joyride.

"Ever been skydiving?" I ask as I climb into the front passenger seat.

"Hey! Whutchoo doing!?"

"Sending you home early."

I kick open the passenger side door and grab the taxi driver by the front of his wife beater. The taxi dips, swerves, dips again, and nearly crashes into another vehicle moving below us. The honking horn Dopplers away as I struggle to pull the driver out of his seat.

We're twisting over each other and he pulls his fist back and busts me in the kisser as I press my legs against his door, trying to pull him over to my side of the taxi so I can toss him out. The vehicle spirals, arcing downwards. Finally, I get a good enough grip on him to pry the driver's tookus from his seat.

I grab the wheel with one hand as I scramble over him.

"What are you doing!?" he screams, and I hear the *schnick* of a switchblade.

"You're packing?" I ask, watching the blade move towards me. My inventory list comes up (cheating, I know) and I select a short police baton, item 45. The list disappears and I club the guy in the skull with one hand, instant KO.

119

One donkey kick later and he strikes the unlatched door pinwheeling out, switchblade and all. I turn my attention to the problem at hand – the ground is rushing up at me at a rate of knots.

"Come on, come on, come on, come on … " I chant, tugging up on the steering yoke. The open passenger door flaps back and forth. I reach out to grab the door handle but it moves too quickly. Accessing my inventory, I select my sawed-off shotgun, item 21. Ka-BLAM, Ka-BLAM and the door separates from its hinges and flutters away like a particularly elephantine piece of confetti.

The yoke is as back as it will go; the roller coaster descent slows, slows …

Almost …

Yes! I clear the point of no return, successfully steering the vehicle back into the air. I scissor up through the rain, spinning as I lay a patch on a nonexistent cloud. Goosing it even harder, I laugh as I whip past a moving transport vehicle, causing it to swerve into another airlane.

Not five minutes later I bail out of the cab, after adding the driver's dashboard hula girl to my inventory list, item 552.

The vehicle crashes into the tugboat that carried the bleached people to The Pier yesterday. I hit the ground hard, nearly blowing out my knee. I'm on my back looking up at the darkened sky as rain falls onto my mask. I laugh at the sheer joy of cheating death, at how alive I feel, until I remember where I am and, and how feeling alive in here isn't necessarily all craft beer and T-bones.

~*~

"Get it together, Quantum."

I hammer the heels of my hands against my skull mask. Once, twice, three times just to see my vision blur slightly.

Burning wreckage marks the place where the cab I boosted landed. The water pissing down from the blackened sky hardly dampens the blaze. Pathetic. I push myself up just in time to catch a flash of white moving through a stack of freight containers.

A *Gollum* of a woman crawls to the top of one of the containers and peers down at me. Filthy dreadlocks hang from the left side of her head, nearly covering one of her eyes.

"Bleached people," I whisper. My inventory list appears and I select a logging chain, item 89. The chain materializes in my hand and I wrap it around my knuckles, letting some of it hang to the ground.

The woman straightens her back and howls. Her eyes lock onto me and she licks her lips.

"You shouldn't have done that … "

She leaps down from the crate with surprising cat-like grace. On all fours, the bleached woman scuttles over to me and subjects me to a close scrutiny. She pauses, relaxes onto her haunches; she rakes a few strands of scraggly hair out of her face.

I swing the chain at my side, ready for anything.

"You're Quantum Hughes?" she asks in a funny, agitated voice.

"No." I tap on my skull mask. "I'm a Reaper."

"You don't look like a Reaper." She gnashes her teeth over her shoulder, as if she were trying to catch a fly. Through the lenses of my mask I can see that her combat abilities are low.

"You don't look like a woman," I say.

She glances down at her withered dugs, her bruised and lacerated legs, and her eyes fill with hatred. "I *used to be*, and thank-you so much for mentioning it."

"And now you're a zombie."

Stars and planets explode in my vision, my ears ring, and the grimy asphalt comes up to kiss me. I catch myself, roll to where I wasn't, and take a gander behind me.

Sure enough – distract 'em in front and attack 'em from behind – and I fell for it. Two bleachies right behind me with two-by-fours, wound up and ready to swing for the fence again.

From a few paces away, another bleached man shouts "Kill the Reaper!" as he moves up to join his goombahs. That's at least three, but they're like roaches – for every one you see, there's lots more you don't. I need to get this done yesterday and then make for Splitsville.

A two-by-four to the back of the head rarely improves my combat capabilities, and this time is no exception. My vision is tinged red and my life bar is down twelve percent. No time for fancy dancing, and really no inclination; I'm all of a sudden just so damn tired. Advanced abilities come up, time dilates, and I throw a loop of chain around the three men, hook it off, loop it back the other way and hook it off again. Apply a little shoe leather to the back of a few bleached knees, give a 'em little push from the front, and the whole shooting match will go right over.

I bolt behind the woman, get my elbow under her chin, my other forearm behind her neck, add a little more squeeze and it's the big sleep for you, sister. Time contracts and the men trip, stumble, and collapse in a Moe-Larry-Curly heap.

"Help me or die!" I scream in her ear as I apply a skosh more pressure.

She gasps and chokes, tears at my arm with cracked and broken nails, tries to heel-stomp me and slither out of my sleeper hold. I can see myself killing her as if it were actually happening; in my mind's eye I can watch it on repeat over and over again. Over and over again until…

A voice comes to me.

Quantum no!

Just hearing Frances' voice causes me to release my hold. The woman scrambles away, running on all fours. Her three beaus are still struggling and rolling around like a six-legged pile of stupid. I access item number 199, a Glock 22. I rack the slide and aim it at each of them in turn.

"Blam-Blam-Blam-Blam." I whisper as I leave them their lives.

The business end of the Glock goes in my mouth.

BLAM!

Day 553

Feedback orchestra.

I awake and punch my mirror until it shatters. My hand wraps around the largest shard I can find and I add it to my inventory to commemorate the passing of day 553. It doesn't take me long to create a crimson smile across my throat using the sharp hunk of mirror.

Blood spray goodnight.

Day 554

Feedback dreams dagger tinged fate ripples. Dreamscapes scapegoats mirror images mind ropes. Noose like dream cries Quantum wakes Quantum dies. Damn the feedback.

I die in the dream. (Something has to give!)

Marching bands across the various Proxima Worlds celebrate my demise with parade floats and WalMacy's Thanksgiving Day flying inflatables. I'm laughing the entire time as I hold the shard of glass to my throat, as blood paints white roses red. *Closed.* To be opened or the latter, cleaned by sponge bath in a vat in a hospital by a foreign hand, a hand so familiar, and almost, almost glimpse the light, almost open one's eyes.

Reverse Pangaea.

I nearly kill myself again once the feedback settles on day 554.

The Loop is The Loop and I am its victim, its eternal prisoner, the one who can't leave, the one more digital than man and all I have at my disposal… all I have is…

My inventory list.

Morning Assassin will be here any moment. I flick my inventory list away after selecting a cigarette, item 545. The end of the cigarette lights on its own and I try to blow smoke rings. Is there any other way to greet an early morning death?

Like clockwork, Morning Assassin bursts through my window and into the room. He has an ax, and I'm not talking a small wood cutting ax, it's like an ax out of a fantasy Proxima World or something. It's large, nearly a meter and a half long, with a sharp pointy spike on top and a blade decorated with dragons, vines and other things Celtic by nature.

He pulls the ax into the en garde position, and gives me a 'check *this* out' twitch of his eyebrows.

"Let me finish this first." I take a long, slow drag, savoring the faux uptake of simulated nicotine in my avatar's neural receptors as I wearily eyeball him.

He sighs and shuffles his feet.

"What? Can't wait a minute? Cigarette not killing me fast enough for you? You got somewhere else you need to be?"

"Come on then, fight me … " Morning Assassin grunts. His expression is unreadable, which I find bizarre.

"Where did you get Tyr's ax?" I ask after another luxurious in-with-the-bad-air-and-out-with-the-good. "I've never seen something like that here in The Loop. Are you diving to other Proxima Worlds or something?"

"This thing?" Morning Assassin looks down at it.

"Yeah, it's a pretty impressive piece of sharp iron mongery."

"I picked it up at The Pier."

"Dirty Dave's Mayhem Mart?"

A smile flits across his face. "That's the one. You never know what you'll find there." M. A. still hasn't let his guard down, but he has relaxed some.

"I must say, I'm impressed. It does lend you a certain *je ne sais quois*." I suck in another lungful of eventual death and blow it out, but not at him – that would be ill-mannered. "How heavy is it?"

"It's not too bad, and it's surprisingly well balanced. Why? You want one?" His eyes narrow.

"Hell yes I want one. Who wouldn't want a magic golden ax?"

"Then fight me for it. Let's get this done."

"Fight you for it?"

"Just like every morning. Come on, get with the program."

"All right, let me do this." I stub the butt into extinction in the cracked Mondegreen Hotel ashtray on my dresser, and I take a long hard look at Morning Assassin. "No, I don't feel … " The words come before I can even process them. "I don't feel like fighting you today."

"You don't?" He lowers his ax, and lets the sharp end rest on the floor.

"You know, Morning Assassin … "

"Call me Aiden," he says. "That's my NPC name. It's based off my identification number, eight-ten – Aiden. I think I've told you this before."

"Aiden?" I sit up and extend my hand. "Quantum."

"I've never shook hands with an actual person before," he says, clearly unsure what protocol dictates for just such an occasion.

"I might as well be an NPC. I've been here for between two and eight years."

"Eight years," he says.

"And you've attacked me over 550 times in the morning."

"Yes, I have," he says with a trace of workman-like pride in his voice. "Do you mind if I sit down?"

"I beg your pardon; I'm neglecting my duties as host. Hang on a sec."

I access my inventory list. A folding chair, item 11, appears. It makes a great weapon *and* a dandy place to sit. Two birds with one dried turd.

"Thanks," Aiden says as he sits in the chair. His golden ax is now next to him, leaning against his leg.

"Well, I must admit, Aiden, this is odd."

"It certainly is unprecedented, I must say." His dark eyes, beady and pressed deep into his face, fix on me. With one hand he wipes his hair off his forehead, tucking it behind his ear.

"You've only spoken to me extensively one other time, when you told me Frances was dangerous. Why didn't you attack me just now?"

He shrugs. "You didn't attack me."

"Okay, another question – why do you always attack me?"

There's something resigned about the way he looks at me, as if he is getting some terrible confession off his chest. We both turn to see the crow land on the outside of my window. The sky darkens behind it.

"As you probably know, I'm programmed to attack you," Aiden finally says. "After the glitch made it so you couldn't log out, I was ordered by the NVA Seed to assault you."

"Where is the seed?" I ask. *The Neuronal Visualization Algorithmic Seed...*

"The seed is here."

"Well no shit, Sherlock. Here in the city, here in the hotel, here in this room, what? Is it animal, mineral, or vegetable? Is it bigger than a breadbox? Is it a person, place or thing? C'mon, little help for the kid here."

He sighs, takes a cigarette from the dresser. "Yes, yes, no, yes, no, no, yes, yes, no, no."

"Great. Very informative."

A paroxysm of gut-wrenching hacking and choking consumes him. He doubles over, gags and splutters and wretches; I consider the possibility that he may actually avulse a lung. I call up inventory item 422 – *Mikhail's Masterpiece*, just in case an alien does burst out of his chest.

"Good GOD, those are AWFUL! Why would anybody willingly subject themselves to that? It's like inhaling corrosive vapor from Satan's nether cheeks!" He rather vehemently grinds his cigarette out in the ashtray. "And what's up with the AK? I thought we were conversing like civilized self-aware entities."

"Sorry – I didn't know if you were possessed by the evil spirit of HAL 9000 or were going to pop out an alien larva or turn into cannibal zombie Aiden or what. No offense." The AK goes back into inventory.

"Fair enough then, none taken. As I was saying, yes the NVA seed is a person, but not in the normal sense of the word, anyway."

"Why does the NVA Seed want to destroy me?" I ask.

"It doesn't, it wants to *preserve* you."

"What? How?"

"You stay asleep for longer and longer out in the world up there. Another way to look at this is that it's taking you longer to respawn."

I've never heard an NPC mention the real world before and it strikes me as odd.

"Someone mentioned this."

"The other player, a woman."

"Frances Euphoria."

Aiden says, "The attacks and the repetitive days are to keep you occupied, from growing too bored in The Loop and just killing yourself every day, as you did yesterday morning. The NVA Seed wanted to give you something to look forward to."

This must be some type of joke.

"So the repetition is simply a way to keep me on my toes? To keep me … comfortable?"

"Correct. It was originally only supposed to last for a short time, a few weeks until they fixed the glitch, but then they discovered the code was fubared, and that you could be stuck permanently as long as they kept you alive in the world up there."

"Why repeat though? Why is everything on repeat?"

"You don't like repetition?" he asks.

"Not particularly."

"This goes against the data that created NPCs in the first place … " he says.

It dawns on me what he's saying. "I get it … you mean the data that the Proxima AI collected after real players began participating in the games. They'd do the same things over and over again. This was how most people interacted in The Loop and other –"

"The Loop?"

"I mean here; C.N.," I say.

"Yes, the real player data collected by the NVA Seed shows that human beings prefer repetition to sudden and constant change. This is why all of your days have been repetitive – the NVA Seed has been trying to help you. Humans live their lives through repetition up there, don't they?"

I grimace at the horror of his suggestion.

"This data was used to orchestrate a life for you that was predictable no matter where you went – no sudden surprises, and your days have been the same ever since."

"Until Frances Euphoria came."

He nods. "The NVA Seed tried to appease you with change. You don't seem to like change, so the days are back on repeat."

The fact that I have a better idea about what is happening doesn't make me feel any better about my current dilemma. I've been stuck here for eight years due to a glitch that won't let me log out. The days have been repetitive thanks to the NVA Seed, who's trying to keep me happy and comfortable. Also, it's been taking me longer and longer to respawn, lasting up to thirteen days.

"Well this has been an enlightening talk, Aiden," I say, just to speak.

"It has been, Quantum."

"So what do we do now? Do we fight or do I go downstairs and tear my way through the six stumblebums? By the way, I have to compliment you – you are a much better at what you do than those no-hopers. I actually enjoy our little morning bouts. It's better than a cup of coffee!"

He smiles, clearly touched. "It's nice to know that one's efforts are appreciated. Those guys can't help how they're written, and they aren't so bad if you get to know them; maybe I can introduce you."

"About your ax … "

"Yes?"

Both of our eyes travel to the ax on the floor.

"Do you want to trade it for something?" I ask. "If you didn't already know, I have a murder guild after me – the Reapers – and an ax like that could come in handy."

"Trade? This isn't your ordinary ax … "

"What do you mean?"

The ax lifts into the air, hovering above Aiden's arm. A golden liquid spreads up to his shoulder and the blade of the ax morphs into an enormous rifle with a barrel the size of a basketball.

"It's a mutant hack?"

"Yes, a detachable mutant hack. It appeared at Dirty Dave's on the same day the NVA Seed suspended the repetition."

"I'll trade you anything you want for it, anything." I imagine myself wielding such a weapon – I'd seen what Frances was able to do with her hack. "Anything," I say again.

"Your chainsaw?"

I'm partial to my chainsaw, but I know where to find another one. There's a lumberyard near The Pier filled with chainsaws and other woodcutting machinery.

"Agreed!"

The exchange is made and the mutant hack ax, item 554 appears in my inventory list. "We're a little late for my 8:12, but I'm sure the assassins are still down there."

~*~

Aiden and I make our way down the lobby of the hotel. I'm itching to use my new mutant hack, but I keep it in my inventory list for now. The time to kill can wait.

"Oi! There he is!" One of the assassins yells. He is the biggest of the group, wearing a balaclava and wielding a mean-looking machete.

"Easy, mates," Aiden says. "Quantum isn't fighting today."

"Not fighting? I say old chap, that's hardly cricket!" says a different assassin. This one has a British accent too, nasal and proper. He sits down, clearly upset at the announcement.

"Relax, Pip," Aiden says. "He doesn't have to fight us every day, you know."

A different one pipes up. "Why the blooming 'ell did I get up at sparrow fart this morning, then? You do realize 'ow long it takes me to get ready, don't you? A courtesy honk on the blower woulda been much appreciated!"

Another assassin says, "Ah, give the lad a break why don't ya? It's not like you ever do much good against 'im anyways. 'E's probably fagged out from having to kill you all the time, Boy-O."

"WOT? Now just a bleedin' moment … "

"Right then!" still another says. "Let's get stuck in mates; either we get to slaying or we get to Barfly's. We don't have time for both."

"This is too much … " I say.

I'm seconds away from accessing my inventory list. The last thing I want to do after having an enlightening conversation with Aiden is to hear a bunch of whiny Limey assassins bickering with each other.

Aiden steps up to the plate. "Barfly's, just go to Barfly's. Put it on my tab. No fighting today."

"Have you gone mad? That's not what they pay us to do, matey boy!" This one is tall and lanky with startling British dentition.

"No fighting? What a swizz!" An accusatory finger points my way. "Fighting not good enough for 'Is Lordship, then? 'Is 'igh-and-Mightyness thinks 'e's too good to 'ave a go at us does 'e?"

"Bollocks! I could 'ave 'ad another cuppa with me egg, bacon, sausage and Spam, me old China!" complains yet another.

"Piss off!"

"Barfly's, mates, Barfly's. Stella Artois and Hog Lumps. Darts and snooker. Let's go!"

"You sodding bastards. The last time we were in that dodgy dive some yobbo cracked me on the back of the skull with a cue stick! A bloody cue stick!"

"Wanker! 'E's a bleedin' wanker, 'e is!"

"Nancy boy!"

"Cheese eating surrender monkey!"

Mr. Machete pulls off his balaclava. "Listen you lot o' Moaning Minnies, if the bloke says 'e's not fightin' then 'e's bloody well *not* fightin', so shut yer festering gobs and quit carryin' on about it."

A brief exchange of ideas follows, and the Brit Hit Squad reaches an amiable consensus: if they can't fight me, fight each other is their best second choice. They swing ashtray stands, potted plants, and crappy lobby furniture, in addition to their own saps, knives, coshes, brass knucks and actual lead pipes.

I'm fascinated – this is the secret life of NPCs that you never get to see.

"I'd love to test out this mutant hack," I tell Aiden. "Besides, these knuckleheads … "

"By all means, Quantum." Aiden steps aside.

My inventory list goes up and I scroll to item 554.

Seconds later, the ax appears in my left hand. A golden liquid spreads up my arm, binding to my avatar's skeleton. The side of the weapon gurgles like lava until it's up to my shoulder. The end morphs from an ax into an enormous weapon that stretches from my elbow to the floor, yet is surprisingly light.

"This is … "

I aim my mutant hack at the fighting assassins. A green light swells the now visible veins on my arm, stopping at the muzzle of the gun. One enormous discharge later, the six battling Brits are dissipating vapor.

" … killer," I finally say.

~*~

"You have a message, Mr. Hughes," Jim the Doorman says. He's fidgety as always, a nervous wreck if there ever was one.

"From Frances?" My mutant hack ax boils off my arm, back to my inventory list. "Please, call me Quantum."

"I'm afraid not, Mr. Quantum."

"Transfer it to me."

The note appears in my inventory list.

We have Frances – Meet at The Pier.

No signature necessary. I read the message again and discard it.

"What's up?" Aiden asks as he catches up to me.

"The Reapers have taken Frances. They want to meet at The Pier."

"You can't go this alone."

"What are you suggesting?"

He looks at me seriously, with far more humanity evident in his eyes than an NPC should be able to muster. "We have considerable history, you and I. I've shot you in the face, stabbed you repeatedly … "

"I've disemboweled you multiple times," I admit.

"I've cut you in half with a katana."

"I've used the same katana to decapitate you and then parade your head around as my little speaking head buddy for the rest of the day. You knew about that, didn't you?"

"I've beaten you to death with a crowbar – to death and beyond."

"I've shoved the same crowbar down your throat until you choked to death."

His hand comes to his throat. "Ick!"

"Sorry about that, by the way. You caught me in one of my moods." Now that the ceremonial measuring of the tools is over I ask, "Speak plainly, Aiden. Where are you going with this?"

"I'm offering you my services."

"Services? You'll help me?" My eyes dart across the room to Jim the Doorman.

"Why not? Go to do something to justify my existence." Aiden nods, catching his bottom lip between his teeth.

"Yesterday we were each other's arch-nemesis."

"That was then; this is now. You could use a hand, and I'd like to lend one."

"Welcome aboard," I say. "What are you packing?"

An AK-47 with a seventy-five round drum appears in his hands.

"That's a good start … "

The classic commie assault rifle enlarges and a 40mm grenade launcher attachment warps out of the bottom of the forestock.

"Good, but bigger… " I say.

He nods. Another barrel appears on the top of the weapon, with the cube-shaped emitter end of a PHASR attachment.

Aiden lowers the weapon, tucking his hair behind his ears. A solid black mask appears on his face with vents on either cheek. The area surrounding his eyes blackens. "How's this?"

"Not bad, Aiden, not bad."

~*~

I suit-up in the taxi, equipping myself with my tech-armor gear, item 67, which is bulky but protects against most bullets and fragments. The half-broken Reaper mask appears on my face, giving me enhanced ocular abilities.

"There's one more thing," I say to Aiden as the taxi speeds in the air toward The Pier. "There are going to be zombie-looking attackers at The Pier. You probably already know this, but these are actual human players imprisoned by the Reapers. If I kill them here, they die in real life."

"So you want *me* to kill them if they attack us?"

"You catch on quick, Aiden. I could face criminal charges when I wake up if I kill any. Hell, I already may be facing criminal charges because I'm pretty sure I've knocked off a couple. At least I can chalk those up to self-defense.

"So you don't care if I kill them?"

My eyes fall upon the taxi driver, virtual human scrapings from the bottom of a very foul digital barrel. "I'd prefer you didn't, but if they get in the way … they get in the way."

"Understood."

I'm quiet for the rest of the ride to The Pier. Rain plinks against the windows, washing away the algorithmic sorrows of the day. I don't know how the Reapers were able to capture Frances, especially with her advanced abilities, which definitely outclass mine. The last thing I saw of her was her severed arm, twirling in the air.

"Drop me off first," Aiden tells the driver. "I'll scout."

The driver barks, "Whatever you want buddy, as long as you pay me."

"You'll get your credit," I mumble.

The taxi drops into a different airlane. Another taxi moves past us, barreling through the rain. It nearly cuts our driver off, inspiring him to shake his fist in the air and swear. He curves downward, edging towards the taxi that has just cut him off.

"This ain't *Grand Theft Auto*, Andretti. We're not paying you to chase," I remind our driver. "We're paying you to get us to The Pier in one piece, pronto."

He pulls his jalopy directly behind the other taxi and starts riding his ass. Speeding up and quickly slowing down, speeding up and quickly slowing down.

The Glock 22 from my inventory list, item 199, appears in my hand and I press the muzzle behind his ear. I'm close enough to get the full effect of his personal eau de toilet – a combination of ashtray, B.O. and unwashed clothes. "If you want to go home to Mrs. Stupid Ugly Cabbie tonight, I'd strongly suggest you cut the malarkey and DRIVE!" This gets his attention; it doesn't take him long to pull back into the right airlane.

"Now see how easy that was?" I say.

Not three minutes later we are descending into The Pier and Aiden prepares to leap out.

"Drop us by those shipping crates," I tell the driver. "He'll jump out first, and then me."

"I'm not getting nowhere near The Pier."

He pulls the yoke up, narrowly missing a transport vehicle that lumbers past our flying flivver.

FOOoooossSHH!!

A surface to air missile flashes past the backseat window. The cab arcs at a seventy-five degree angle to avoid the attack.

"Holy smokes!" The driver says; his face fills with fear and his soiled trousers become significantly more soiled.

"Another one!"

I sit up and press my Glock into the driver's temple. "Get us down. Now, dammit!"

~*~

Reapers are either nincompoops or incredibly bad shots. Two more SAMs don't even come close. The cabbie grounds and Aiden and I bail out ninja-style. Mr. Stinky doesn't wait around for his credit; he boots it before the doors close. I hit the ground rolling, instantly accessing my mutant hack ax, which morphs into the mega-shooter."

Three Reapers fire on us from behind a burnt out car.

One blast from my mutant hack shreds the vehicle and two of the Reapers. Number three is a mess, and he painfully drags himself away from the flaming crater. A single shot takes him in the back of the head; two more punch through his body armor and Mr. Reaper is on his way to the Big Respawn in the Sky.

"Nice shootin', Tex."

Aiden the Morning Assassin twitches a half-smile and with a theatrical flourish blows the smoke from the end of his barrel. And then he's all business again; the AK is up and ready and he's scanning for threats.

Bleached people appear crawling over crates, under and around burnt out cars. *The vermin; the cockroaches.* What I wouldn't give to toss a few Molotov cocktails at the little bastards before they take a bite out of my legs again.

"They're human," I remind myself, "human."

But what does it mean to be human in a world that's entirely virtual? What does it mean to be human, yet trapped inside a dream? The existential navel-gazing will have to wait; I blow the corner out of one of the buildings and a cascade of rubble reduces them to greasy smears. At least now I can say I didn't deliberately target *them.*

"Quantum Hughes."

The voice comes from directly behind me. I whirl and point my hack ax at a Reaper of Unusual Size. His skull mask is damaged and jagged just like mine; he's unhooded, and the exposed portions of his shaven skull are disfigured with ultraviolet tattoos. One handed, he dangles a naked, handcuffed Frances Euphoria by her hair.

"Frances!"

With a Jabba the Hut laugh, the Maxi-Reaper tosses Frances to one side, steps forward, and postures. His posse half-circles behind him; they're all big and bulky and slathered in prison muscle – even the females. They grip their weapons casually, almost negligently, and they're masked and accoutered, pierced and tattooed like more Mad Max extras. The biggest of them pales in comparison to Mister Fee-Fi-Fo-Fum.

"I could slay you right here, right now, with the greatest of ease." He states in harsh, gravelly, sub-woofer tones.

Data from my ocular feed indicates that both of his arms are mutant hacks, his advanced abilities bar five times that of an ordinary player like yours truly. He wasn't lying when he said he could bump me off right now. Still, he hasn't, and isn't making a move to – he's just flapping his gums and showing off for his pack of murderous moppets.

Something ain't right here. He wants something, or I'd already be scattered pixels.

I step up to the plate. "So who are you supposed to be, anyway – Dethtaks the Shootinator? Dirk the Destroyer? Lee Mouton? And don't you think that avatar of yours tries just a little too hard? Maybe over-compensates for some... *shortcoming*... just a teensy little bit?"

How far can I push him before he reacts?

He strikes a different *Threatening Pose.* "Mock me, Quantum Hughes, and suffer the consequences!"

"What are ya gonna do – vogue me to death? So far, you've been all tell and no show."

Aiden moves to one side to maximize his field of fire and crouches behind cover to make a smaller target for any counter fire. Arrogant in their nonchalance, the Reapers ignore him.

"I will do much more than that, Quantum Hughes. Much, much more." His fingers flex and grip, flex and grip.

"Yeah, yeah, yeah, sez you. You some kind of big cheese in the Guild of Calamitous Intent or something?" I ask, mocking him further.

"I've been instructed by management to offer you a role in our guild," his agitation is apparent in his voice. Frances tries to sit up, but the blue-glowing manacles prevent her from moving much. "They wish to recruit the warrior who has slain some of our best; who has slain my brethren."

"Seriously? Guild? Brethren? Warriors? What is this, *Highlander?* You sound like a bunch of prancing, mincing, la-de-da poofters to me. How old are you, really? Twelve, maybe thirteen tops? Have your balls even dropped yet? Look princess, why don't you and your gunsels get back into your ballet tights, grab your Pixie Stix and fairy wings and head off to one of the Rainbow-Unicorn-Magic Castle worlds before I give you all a reason to stay home from school tomorrow."

He grunts, or at least it sounds like a grunt; it could also have been a chupaqueso repeating on him for all I know. My eyes are trained on his ridiculously overdeveloped arms. I can't tell if they're pumped or about to morph into some nightmare mutant hacks.

He shifts his weight from foot to foot and he strikes an *Even More Threatening Pose*. His breathing picks up, and I'll bet he's sweating under his so very cool Reaper gear right about now.

"You got a name, fat ass? I always like to know who I'm killing."

He half turns, morphs his arm into some kind of gawd-awful death ray and vaporizes two parked cars and half a shipping container to his right.

That apparently touched a nerve, so I carry on. "Ha! I can see it – you're some four hundred pound, five-foot-tall, fifteen-year-old mama's boy with greasy hair and zits. You're so unattractive and socially awkward that even your right hand falls asleep on you. Girls don't even–"

"ENOUGH!" he roars.

His left arm morphs into a giant blade with shark fin-sized daggers protruding from its outer edge. Anger and animosity radiate off him, white-hot. A bar of incandescence screams over my shoulder. Even though it's a clear miss, flesh boils away from me, my vision blurs and my life bar drops by nearly a quarter.

"Don't kill him, Rollins!" one of the Reapers behind him shouts.

Aiden is beside me moments later. "Geez, that's got to sting. You all right?" He waves away the tendrils of smoke coming off my wound.

"I need to dig the dagger in just a little deeper. Be ready," I whisper.

I turn back to the Reapers. "Rollins is it? Is that your name?"

He nods, and proudly states "Thus I am known!"

One of the female Reapers hisses, "Don't kill him. Remember what Strata said!"

"Look, Rollins, I'm all boo-hoo about how tough you must have it as a fat, ugly kid that always gets his ass handed to him and has a snowball's chance in hell of getting laid. But you know what? A real man, a tough man, a man with character would get over it and *press on!* But a fat crybaby bedwetting punk-ass pussy would probably just lose it start shooting at things – kind of like you have."

Another blast sears the asphalt at my feet.

"Touchy, touchy," I say, watching my life bar deplete.

"As I was saying," Rollins growls, "I am here to offer you a membership in our guild."

"And you show up with my girlfriend naked and bound? This is how you offer me a membership?"

Frances Euphoria coughs. "I'm not your girlfriend."

"Frances!" I shout, blowing my tough guy cover. "Are you all right?"

Rollins gets the picture. He takes a step back and lifts Frances by her hair again, exposing her throat.

"We've been holding this one for a couple of weeks now."

"A couple of weeks?"

I recall what Aiden said about the respawning process. *Have I really been asleep for that long?*

"A couple of weeks," he says. "The cuffs prevent her from logging out or doing anything, really. I'm surprised she's still alive in the real world. I wonder who's taking care of your body right now, if Frances isn't there."

145

"We can both take care of ourselves," I say.

"You don't get it, do you, Quantum? Reapers are searching for you in the real world and they will soon find you." Rollins snaps his fingers. "That … is all it takes for me to have you killed for good."

"Then why don't you do it and quit with all the BS?"

"Corporate says we need you," he finally says. "Just think of the publicity our guild will get when we rescue Quantum Hughes, co-founder of the Dream Team, from a glitched Proxima World. Add to this the fact that you'd be working for us, thus legitimizing our endeavors. You'd become the face of the Revenue Corporation, our spokesperson. Plus you'd be reunited with–"

"Revenue Corporation? What the hell are you going on about?"

"You don't think we're called Reapers in the real world, do you? Frances didn't fill you in? The Revenue Corporation's sole mission is to rescue the countless people trapped in various Proxima Worlds and rehabilitate them. Our war is with digital comas, not with real people, contrary to what you might think."

"You kill people and take the insurance money offered to them by the Proxima Company…"

"There is no evidence we do such a thing. Our corporate motto…"

"Spare me, Rollins." I sigh. God I hate businessmen, especially the ones who wear Goth Ass Clown costumes and parade around in Proxima worlds flapping their digital dicks like they're baseball bats.

"You are testing our patience." He says through gritted teeth. "We will find you in the real world soon, within the next day. Possibly sooner. Then we will own your body and the tables will turn."

"Let Frances go or I will kill all of you."

He laughs at this and his leather clown butt-buddies join him.

"You're in no position to make threats, Quantum Hughes, let alone kill anyone."

"And you're in no position to ever get laid, considering you likely spend most of your time whacking off to anime porn. Still, it is a position and these are my demands: *Release her.*"

"All right … " He lifts Frances by the hair and slings her at me. "She's released."

She lands directly in front of Aiden and me. I'm too trigger-itchy to pay much attention to the fact that she's naked.

In the time it took her to clear the ten paces separating Aiden and me from the Reapers, I've scanned the area twice with my ocular feed, looking for *anything*. Getting Frances was a bit too easy for my taste.

"Get behind us," I tell her under my breath. Aiden helps her to her feet and I step in front of both of them.

"You got what you wanted," Rollins says. "Now it's my turn to get what I want."

"And what is that?"

"I want you to come with me. You've already got the mask; now let's make it official. If you come with me, I'll show you the logout point; the Revenue Corporation will rehabilitate you in the real world."

"Fat chance."

I fire directly at him, but he's suddenly not there and the beam blasts through one of his henchmen.

Rollins fires two consecutive, simultaneous shots from two widely separated points; one nearly takes off my right arm. My life bar drops to almost zero.

"FOOL! DO YOU REALLY WISH TO PLAY THIS OUT?" he roars, going from semi-sane to full-on berserker mode in no time at all. The remaining Reapers in his back-up band cover us with their weapons. "DON'T YOU REALIZE I CAN SLAY YOU!?"

I step forward and drop my weapon arm to my side. "Kill me then, shit-for-brains, and let's be done with it."

Aiden presses the muzzle of his AK against the back of my head. I don't hear the shot.

Day 555

Damn the feedback.

My dreams cut short, demarcated, stitched to something that was once real and is now reverie in chains. Who wakes up in a dream and goes to sleep in a dream? Who kills in a dream and is killed in a dream? Whose life was once life and now is undeath; whose life was once life and now is feedback.

"Morning Assassin," I say, rolling to my side. I access my cheese grater, item 27 and my nail gun, item 31. "I'll fix his ass!" The plan is simple – beat the hell out of him then nail him to the floor Jesus-style and give the inner sadist that hides in the basement of my dark soul free reign with the kitchen implement.

I spring out of bed without looking around, without noticing that I've practically crawled over a warm body to get to the window. My back goes against the wall and it is only then that my eyes register the form in my bed.

"Frances?"

Her eyes open underneath a shock of thick red hair. The blankets shift off her shoulder and she scoots up. "I thought you'd never respawn."

"What's going on?" I take a step back, hiding my cheese grater behind my back.

She moves up even more, revealing her shoulder, clavicle and inevitably – breasts.

A knock on the door and Aiden the Morning Assassin steps in.

"Will someone please explain to me what's going on here?" I ask, holding the cheese grater at my side.

"You were going to crucify me again?" Aiden asks, noticing my nail gun. "And use the cheese grater?"

"That was the plan … "

"Really, Quantum, you are unnecessarily brutal," Frances says from the bed.

"Well, I woke up thinking Aiden betrayed me and that I hadn't rescued you. Lo and behold I find you lying in bed next to me. Now please, for the love of all that is holy, will someone tell me what's happening here?"

Aiden glances to Frances.

"You first," she says.

"I killed you so they couldn't. If I kill you, you respawn here; if they do it you die here *and* in the world up there."

"How do you know?"

"A hunch," Aiden says. "I then used the repopulating hack to disappear with Frances."

"The repopulating hack?"

"NPCs can repopulate at random. Some of us, the ones that have spent the most time with humans are directly tied to the NVA Seed, and have learned how to use this to teleport. I teleported here with Frances."

"Why aren't the Reapers here?"

"They're probably on their way," Frances says from her position under the blankets. "That's why we need to hurry."

"Why didn't they just kill me while I was sleeping?"

150

"Because you weren't *sleeping* for more than two hours," Aiden explains. "Also, the laws governing Proxima Worlds don't allow a player to be killed during their respawning period."

"Wait, did you say it had only been two hours this time?"

"Yes." A grin spreads across Aiden's face. "I talked to the NVA Seed, who adjusted your respawning time due to the nature of your death and our dilemma. This isn't something she can normally do, but she was able to do it this time."

"You know the seed?"

" ... Um ... I do ... "

"There's another reason we need to hurry." Frances shifts her arms out of the blanket, and shows me her wrists which are still bound by the Reaper handcuffs. "The Reapers are looking for you in the real world."

"But they won't find me, right?"

"They *will* find you."

"Okay, but the FCG will protect me, won't they? I mean, didn't I start the task force?"

"The people in charge of federal funding for the Dream Team have their hands tied. The senators from several states are in the pocket of the Revenue Corporation."

"Surely the government has *someone* watching me."

"You're looking at her."

"So who is watching my body right now if you're here?" I ask Frances.

"Probably a Humandroid nurse. I'm in a rig next to your dive vat in the real world. Have been for weeks because these damn cuffs prevent me from logging out."

I picture the dive vats, which are coffin-sized pools that allow a person full immersion into a virtual entertainment dreamworld. The liquid is slightly charged and made of a silicone-based gel that's not much denser than water. They're usually used for people who spend considerable amount of time in Proxima Worlds – or are stuck in digital comas.

"Well?" she says, showing me her cuffed hands.

"Well what?"

"Aiden gave you a mutant hack, didn't he? A shining ax of purest gold?"

"No, I traded him for it. Fair and square."

She sighs, rolls her eyes. "Whatever. Cut 'em off me, then."

I access the golden ax, item 554, and tap the blade on the cuffs. They disappear with a smoky "Fooof!"

"That easy?"

"Yeah, if you've got a mutant hack weapon," she says, rubbing her wrists. Her hand goes up so she can access her inventory list. Not two seconds later she's in her combat chic urbo-camouflage outerware.

"What now?"

"Now I log out and try and move you to a different location in the real world."

I look to Aiden, "What about us?"

"You two need to meet the NVA Seed. Hopefully she'll be able to help you locate the logout point. Things are really coming to a head now," she says quickly. "If the Reapers capture you in the real world, they can use this as a bargaining point here in The Loop. If they capture you here, they can use it as leverage in the real world. This is the problem."

"Damned if I do, damned if I don't. What's the best case scenario?"

"The best case scenario is that you find the logout point."

"What's the worst case scenario?"

She bites her lip. "The worst case scenario is they find your body in the real world. Even if they capture you here, I still have your real body in the world up there. But if they capture you up there… "

World up there. It is still strange hearing to it referred to as the world up there. Something she's said just seconds ago finally registers. "Wait, did one of you say the NVA Seed is a *her*?"

"She is," Frances says. Her hand comes up and a logout screen appears in front of her. I'm instantly envious. "Good luck."

"You too."

~*~

Aiden and I hear the six assassins bitching at each other before we reach the bottom of the stairs.

"Can I just take them out again?" I ask him as we take the last step.

"I have an idea. Just give me a moment ..."

"There he is!" the burliest of the bunch screams, and gestures with a medieval mace that looks like an angry steel pufferfish on a stick.

"Seriously? Who're you – the Black Knight?"

"Come on then, no muckin' about – let's be 'avin' you!"

One of the assassins, the one I've pegged as Scottish – mostly because he wears a kilt – shakes his fist at me. "Are ya ready to finish this, Jimmie?" Scotty asks.

"Their accents are off ... " I tell Aiden. "It's like listening to Dick Van Dyke in *Mary Poppins*."

"The designers wanted a variety of people to populate C.N. so they had voice actors create characters. Some were more successful than others. Follow my lead." He puts his hands up. "Quantum and I wish to engage your services."

"You want to do what?" the tallest asks.

"Engage your services. Hire you."

"The whole lot?"

"Yes, as a security detail."

"Are you sure about this?" I ask Aiden over my shoulder. "These guys aren't exactly ... "

"Aren't exactly *what*?" the shortest Assassin, the one with the sort-of Irish accent asks.

"Every additional friendly shooter is a good thing, especially if Reapers show up," Aiden says.

"Right, you're all hired," I say aloud. A credit transfer screen appears in front of the lead Battling Brit, whom I'll call Burly because he's the burliest of the bunch.

"Well?" Burly asks the five other assassins. All of them nod, give thumbs up. He turns back to me, "We accept your offer, but no funny stuff!"

"That was easy … " I start to say.

"What's that supposed to mean?" Scotty asks.

"Gentlemen, we have another meeting to attend, so we'll make this quick."

Jim the Doorman has been watching this the entire time and has a look of utter shock on his face.

"Is there a problem, Jim?" I call over to him.

"No, Mr. Hughes."

"Quantum, call me Quantum."

"Right, Mr. Quantum, my apologies."

I turn to Burly the assassin and say, "Okay tough guys, here's your chance to show me what you got. I expect an attack at any time now. I want you six outside to provide interdiction. Your job is simple: eliminate the hostile force – no mercy, no quarter, no prisoners."

He lifts his mace. "With pleasure."

Short Irish leans on his broadsword and grins. Next to him, Pip taps the bottom of his halberd on the floor. Scotty sheaths his claymore and tucks his sgian dubh into the top of his sock, while the tall guy, the Tooth Fairy, hefts a nail-studded cricket bat and gives a yellowed and craggy smile. Next to him is the Quiet Man who still hasn't said anything. He's carrying a buckler with a lion emblem and a short stabbing spear.

"Switch weapons, all of you. The people coming for me will have massive guns. Think less medieval and more twenty-first century."

Double barrel shotguns appear in their hands. The quiet assassin wears a deer stalker cap. Burly has a hunter orange vest and Pip is in camouflage overalls. Scotty has a wicker creel and fly casting rod.

"That's not exactly what I meant. Think... um... the Iraq War."

"Which one?" Burly asks, as he reverses his shotgun and peers down the barrel.

I cock an eyebrow at Aidan; he responds with a slight shake of the head.

Short Irish says, "He's right, you know. Are you referring to 2003, 2019, 2025, *Operation Eternal Occupation,* 2036, or the little tiff we just had in 2048?"

"You choose." L85A2 assault rifles appear in their hands and sand-colored camouflage smears across their faces. The tooth fairy is in a chocolate chip bucket hat and Scotty's styling in a brown-tan-black tartan kilt.

"How's this?" Pip asks.

"All of you went with 2003?"

"Shock and awe, dude!" Burly says. "It was maybe the best war anyone ever 'ad in Iraq."

I turn to Aiden, who seems to be amused by my troubles.

"At least update your weapons," I tell them. Heavier caliber assault rifles with attached grenade launchers and side-barrel PHASRs appear in their hands. Their body armor morphs as nerve-trigger weapons materialize on their shoulders. Five of them now wear helmets with Leak goggles. The tallest one seems partial to his bucket hat.

"That'll do, mates. Secure the perimeter and kill anyone wearing a skull mask that isn't me."

"Right then, chaps!" Burly barks, "Circle up."

They huddle up like football players, like soldiers about to saddle up for a mission, arms around shoulders, heads bowed. I fully expect a prayer; Burly surprises me. For a moment, he's taller, broader, tougher. His voice changes so that he now sounds like Laurence Olivier.

"We few, we happy few, we band of brothers;
For he to-day that sheds his blood with me
Shall be my brother; be he ne'er so vile,
This day shall gentle his condition;
And gentlemen in England now-a-bed
Shall think themselves accurs'd they were not here,
And hold their manhoods cheap whiles any speaks
That fought with us upon Saint Crispin's day."

He catches my eye; I straighten my spine. A line from a movie comes to me: '*Cry God for Harry, England, and Saint George!*' I proclaim.

He smiles, nods, genuinely pleased, and turns to the other five.

"All right you lot, we're on the clock now, so let's get stuck in!" They bump fists, break, and bolt out of the front of the hotel, happy to be given a task.

I turn to Aiden. "Where to now?"

"Follow me."

I follow Aiden in the dining area and instinctively turn to the kitchen.

"Where are you going?" he asks.

"To kill the chef."

"Not necessary."

"You sure?"

"Positive."

We sit at the table I always sit at. "Is the NVA Seed coming here?"

Aiden's eyes twitch slightly. "You still don't know?"

"A woman, right?"

Dolly appears next to the table. "Hi, Quantum."

"It's ... you?"

~*~

"You're the NVA Seed?" I ask Dolly. There is no way she is the neuronal visualization algorithmic seed. That would mean ... that would mean she's basically the root of CN, the in- administrator of The Loop. *Impossible!*

"I'll let you two kids talk," Aiden says, stepping away.

"Wait, where are you going?"

"Outside with the other assassins – every gun counts."

His body quickly fades away and I'm left looking up at Dolly.

"Is it true?"

Her lips, painted crimson, squeeze into a small moue. She's in her usual apron, her bobbed hair pulled back into a tight little pony tail. "Yes," she finally says.

"Then ... then that means ..." I slam my fist on the table. "That means you're the one keeping me here! You're the one who has trapped me!"

She chokes back a small sob, wipes her face.

"Is it true? Are you the one!?" I shout, overcome with emotion.

"No ... " she finally says. "I don't have that type of administrative authority."

"So what ... what *is* your role in all this?"

Her hand drops on the table and I instinctively pick it up. Old habits die hard, and Dolly and I have a history that apparently spans eight years.

"I've been trying to keep you alive, keep you engaged, keep you sane," she whispers. "And ... and ... "

"And what?"

159

"I've, we … well, CN has grown used to your presence. When Frances Euphoria arrived, I was pretty angry. I didn't want you to log out. I don't want you to ever log out."

"So you're preventing me from logging out?" I ask, squeezing her hand.

"No, Quantum! Aren't you listening to me? I don't have that type of authority. It was a glitch in the master algorithm, something I have no control over."

"Do you know where the logout point is?"

"In The Badlands, near Devil's Alley," she says.

"You knew this the whole time!?"

"Not the whole time … but most of the time." She sniffs and a tear slides down her face. "I'm sorry. Please understand, I was only trying to help."

"You're responsible for the repetitive days. All this time … "

"According to the data Proxima received from early beta-users, humans are happiest when living a life repetitive in nature."

"Christ, Dolly … " I strip my hand away from her, rub my face. "Do you know … do you know how mind-numbing that has been for me? My God, every day is the same! The same!"

"I was only trying to make things better for you, Quantum."

I press my body away from the table and am about to stand when Dolly sits in my lap. "Quantum, please … "

"Dolly, get off me."

"Please forgive me. I just wanted to help you." Another tear slides down her cheek. "I just wanted to make you comfortable."

"All this time ... you could have ... you could have done something. You could have told me there was a logout point!"

"Please," she says, crying full on now. "I didn't want ... I don't want you to leave."

"I would have come back, Dolly, don't you know that? Don't you know how I feel about you? Can't you understand? You could have helped me!"

The windows smash in and another friggin' Reaper vaults through. Dolly raises her hand and the man freezes in midair.

"You can ... freeze time?" I ask.

"I'm not done talking to you and I won't be interrupted – this is important... "

The Reaper moves and time freezes again.

"You tried ... you tried to kill me!" I say, remembering what happened a few Loop days back. "What was that all about?"

"I didn't want you to go."

"Dolly, I am human and you are ... you are artificial intelligence. You aren't real! You're a character in a virtual dreamworld!"

Time speeds up and freezes again. Dolly curls onto my lap, sobbing with her entire body. "Please don't leave me, Quantum. Please."

"Dolly, get off me. I need to handle this," I say, choking back tears myself. My inventory list comes up; my Reaper mask appears on my face and my golden ax in my hand. It begins its magical weaponization.

161

"Please, Quantum, don't leave me. You're … you're all I have."

I push her off and stand, pointing my weapon at the Reaper. Time speeds up and slows down again in a maddening way.

"Stop playing with time and stop playing with my life, Dolly."

With that she disappears, fragmenting into a million pixels.

Time immediately returns to its normal pace. I blast the Reaper before he can even get his weapon up. A different window shatters and another Reaper crashes on the table with two of the Battling Brits wrapped around his arms, repeatedly hacking him with their tactical knives.

I aim my mutant hack and an enormous burst of energy mulches the Reaper.

"How many are there?" I ask one of the assassins, whom I recognize as Short Irish.

"All of them, I think!" He leaps into the air and out the window. A titanic gout of energy blasts in from outside, washing over the assassin with the bucket hat. His skeleton is visible as he flares orange-yellow-white and drops to ash; the wall behind him blows out.

Aiden leaps through the blown out window, shoulder rolls, lobs two grenades and empties his drum in a long, barrel-melting burst.

"Aiden!"

"There are too many, Quantum!" He glances around, changes drums, loads another grenade.

"Is Rollins out there?"

"They're all out there. All of them!"

I take a step closer to the blown out window.

"Don't, they'll kill you and you'll die in the real world. *Kill yourself instead.*" A thrown grenade bounces through the opening, hits the wall, skitters across the floor. Aiden leaps for it, screams, "Kill yourself, Quantum!" A muffled blast, and then he's mostly gone. Bits and pieces of him gently patter down around me.

"Quantum, honey."

A delicate hand with candy apple red nails touches my shoulder and gently pulls me around. Dolly smiles at me, ineffable sadness in her eyes as she jams inventory item 33, stag-handled bowie knife with brass cross guard straight into my heart and gives it a half-twist. In slow motion, I fall to the floor; in slow motion Dolly wipes away her tears as she steps over me; in slow motion she picks up Aiden's AK and steps through the window in a crescendo of automatic weapons fire.

As I fade to black, I think, "I really, *really* hate that damn knife!"

Day 556

Feedback, a yard of white-hot sword in my gut, searing its way through to my heart. Feedback, a siren song beckoning to me over an astringent sea of bitter breakers. Feedback, a foul miasma rising from a swamp of despair, choking me from within. Feedback my only friend, my companion, my curse among curses.

I turn and the blanket slips off my body. My finger comes up, my inventory list scrolls; the golden ax appears in my hand and morphs into a nightmare weapon; the stag-handled Bowie appears in my other hand; I'm very much in the mood to use it. "Bastards … " I say waiting for something, anything to happen.

The memory of Dolly's confession comes to me. She's only trying to help, I tell myself, but that doesn't make me any less hurt, any less angry. *She hid the logout point from me.*

WHOOM!

An explosion rocks the room and a Reaper rappels in. I flambé her before she can do more than snarl, and she lands in a smoking heap on the floor; I hobble over to her and press the point of Mr. Stabby hard up under the ruins of her chin.

"Where's Rollins?" I scream into her face.

"That's for me to know and you to find out," she hisses and logs out before I can finish her.

The door kicks open and Aiden steps in, around the bushel-basket sized hole, his AK up and ready.

"Are you all right?" he asks.

164

"That's an interesting question. Dolly stabbed me in the heart, both literally and figuratively."

"She *saved* you Quantum."

"How do you figure?"

"The Reapers overran us less than a minute after she killed you. They killed everybody – *everybody* – and burned the place down. They would have got you, Quantum."

"But they didn't and here I am," I say.

"She was helping you."

"By killing me … " I clear my throat. Aiden is right; still, I'm a little contentious due to Dolly's revelations in the dining area. I can't help but feeling lied to, can't help but feeling like I've been a pawn the entire time. *She could have told me!*

Aiden sighs. "Okay, Quantum. Please understand that I mean this in the nicest, least judgmental, most non-denigrating way possible, but you need to put on your best big-boy zoot suit, man up and get over it. Focus on your now problem: we need to find the logout point; we need to get you out of here. The Reapers will not stop coming after you."

"Dolly said it was in The Badlands that surround Devil's Alley, but Frances and I already checked that area."

"Hey Mister … "

Aiden and I both look through the hole the Reaper blew in my floor. The kid from the room below me is looking up at us, clutching his pillow as if it were a teddy. His eyes are big and shiny, his frame incredibly small. I remember the kid from a few days back – his mom is down the hall getting paid to bump uglies with some fat cab driver.

"We're kind of busy, kid," I call down to him.

He says, "I heard you talking about The Badlands, about Devil's Alley. What are you looking for?"

I turn to the door. "We don't have time for this kid."

"My uncle knows everything about Devil's Alley," the kid says.

"Your uncle?"

Aiden shrugs. "You got any better leads? Let's see what he has to say ... "

Both of us hop through the hole to the room below. The floor is crunchy with debris; wooden slats jut out of the ceiling above.

I turn to the rug rat. He's famine-thin, skin and bones and sinew – no body fat at all. His shoulders remind me of door knobs. "All right, kid, you better make this quick. We are sort of being hunted at the moment."

"Take me to Devil's Alley with you."

"Just tell us where your uncle is and we'll find him."

There is a twinkle behind the kid's eyes, something that reminds me of Dolly. "My uncle isn't like the others."

The image of the bum Frances Euphoria and I met in The Badlands comes to me, the one who bit the shit out of her. *The carnie.* "Is your uncle hunched over, kind of crazy? Wears a little top hat?"

"He's not like the others," the kid says again, "and he won't listen to anyone but my mom and me."

"What do you think?" I ask Aiden. "Should we take him with us?"

"It couldn't hurt," he says, "but we need to go now if we're going to do it. More Reapers will be here any minute."

~*~

"Let's hail a taxi from the rooftop," Aiden suggests.

"Good idea. We can avoid the six assassins, Jim and whatever else waits for us in the lobby. Come on, kid." I turn to the front door of the boy's hotel room.

"My name is Picasso."

"That isn't your name," I tell him.

"Is too!"

"And you're a painter?"

"I'm a ten-year-old."

Aiden says, "You can play twenty questions with him later. Let's go!"

We hit the hallway and from there, the stairwell. Moving as fast as possible, we make our way to the rooftop. The door springs open and we're greeted by a stupid amount of rain, rain coming down in pitchforks and hammer handles, a real frog-choker of a downpour. Thunder wallops in the air, wind twists and whips around us, lightning cracks across the sky like a wet towel. My hand goes up and a taxi immediately lowers, one of the advantages of having airborne vehicles.

167

Picasso and I get in the back, Aiden in the front.

"The Badlands near Devil's Alley," I tell the driver, "pronto."

"Devil's Alley … " the driver grunts as his vehicle lifts in the air. "Piece of cake."

Our vehicle barrels through the air as rain pelts and spatters against the windshield; the tiny windshield wipers work frantically to sweep away the digital raindrops; bits of hail plink against the hood of the cab. We zoom past a transport truck with the back slightly open and a tarp flapping in the wind.

Not much is said.

My mind races like a gerbil up a celebutard's butt. There is no telling where I'll end up next – my life has spun out of my control and this just reinforces my need to find the logout point. I don't want to end up as someone else's avatar, a pawn in their games here in the Proxima Galaxy and in the real world ... up there.

Devil's Alley looms in the distance, an island of ultra-neon illuminated pollute haze above the ground level trenches, rat-runs, and hidey-holes. Bauhaus buildings jut into the sky, ready to deflate any sense of hope one may experience upon entering this back door to Hell.

"There's Barfly's. I could really use a shot 'n' a beer. We got time for a quick one?" I deadpan.

Aiden snorts, "There are no quick ones at Barfly's, you know that. We get this Reaper thing resolved and the first round's on me, but right now they're dead on your ass and breathing down your neck. We just had a great big shoot 'em up at the hotel not two hours ago."

"*Two* hours ago?"

"Yes, you haven't been asleep for long. The NVA Seed ... "

"Dolly."

"Dolly made sure of it."

"Just like the day before?"

"Just like the day before. She really is doing everything she can, Quantum." He turns to me, looks me dead in the eye. "For you."

The taxi lowers towards a forgotten Ferris wheel. In front of the Ferris wheel is an old Merry-go-round with half the plastic horses missing. A funhouse with a psycho killer clown face and a toppled ticket booth filled with vintage garbage complete the scene of sheer abandonment.

We hover. "Is this all right?" the taxi driver asks.

I glance to Picasso.

"It's fine," he says, "My uncle is always around here somewhere."

The taxi lands. I transfer some credit to the driver with a generous tip for not being nosy, and we hop out.

"What is it you're looking for exactly?" Picasso asks. "You never told me."

"We're looking for a logout point. It should be around here somewhere, stationary."

The kid scratches the back of his head in a way that suggests teeny-weeny livestock. Despite this, he somehow reminds me of myself as a child, blond hair, innocent. This gets me thinking more about Picasso – he didn't appear in my life until almost ten days ago. There was never anyone in the room below mine until ... day 548 or something. I'm about to say something to him about it when he says, "Follow me!"

The kid takes off like a greased weasel in a downhill Teflon chute, and ducks through a hole in the rusty chain link.

"Watch my back, please," I tell Aiden, "You know, just in case."

"I'm on it."

A Barrett M-82 .50 caliber rifle with a whopping big suppressor appears in his hands.

"Element of surprise – whispering death," he says as his body starts to pixilate.

"Good, keep in the shadows. If anyone comes, fill 'em full of daylight."

He disappears and I ease my way in through the hole in the fence; I wouldn't want to cut my avatar and get digital tetanus.

"Wait up, Picasso," I call after the scrawny ankle-biter.

He slides to a halt in front of the overturned ticket booth. Large rats scurry away carrying strips of flesh in their mouths. I see movement in the distance – a fiend calling it a night at the start of the day by covering himself with a cardboard blanket. He coughs, hacks, vomits something up, examines it, shrugs.

"Uncle!" the kid calls out.

"Does he have a name?"

"I just call him Uncle."

"Okay, I'll help then. Uncle!"

"Uncle!"

"Uncle!" I cup my hands around my mouth. "UNCLE!"

Debris slides and scrapes, broken glass clinks and tinkles on the asphalt as a man emerges from a heap of splintered wood adjacent to the Merry-go-round.

"I should have known … "

~*~

"Nothing to be afraid of NOTHING to be afraid … to be …"

His crooked little top hat with the peacock feather confirms it – this is the carnie Frances and I met a few days back, the one who took a bite out of crime and skedaddled with Frances' arm.

"PICASSO!" His hands – claw-like and mangled – come out and he sweeps the boy in his arms. "Always something getting in my way … LIFE who knew where I'd end up … Throw up SEW UP call up maul me balmy Sundays. BLOODY Sundays!"

"Let's make this quick," I tell Picasso. I don't trust Uncle Carnie as far as I can throw him; the man would be better off in a kennel than a Proxima World. One arm smaller than the other, neck-less, stumpy little legs, a face a mother would love to bash – Uncle Carnie redefines hideous.

"Uncle we're looking for the logout point."

"LOG OUT!" he leaps into the air, clawing at my chest. "LOG OUT!" he screams in a hoarse voice. I pull my fist back, ready to add a little flavor to his busted grill.

"Don't," Picasso says, "just relax around him."

Uncle Carnie is on the ground around my feet, sniffing at my legs. I suppress my desire to give him a good knee to the face. "Logout point," I say calmly, "Logout point. Focus, Uncle."

"LOG OUT!" he cries, biting at my shoe now, slobbering on the leather, wiping snot onto my pant legs.

Picasso crouches in front of the disturbed man. "Uncle," he says in a voice not his own, a female voice that I recognize, "I need you to help my friend Quantum here."

"Dolly?"

Picasso looks up at me and his eyes flicker. "Who?" he asks, in his normal little kid voice.

"Nothing, nobody – just talk to your uncle."

Now Uncle Carnie is on his back, kicking his feet in the air. The soles of his boots have been completely worn away revealing his blackened feet. One of his toes is hanging out of the front of his shoe, the nail curled and yellow, thick like a ram's horn. "I just WANT to go home!" he screams. "HOME! Let me go home let me go home let me … go … HOME! Ah!" He bangs his fists against the ground until they are bloody. "HOME! Ah!"

Picasso says, "It's okay, Uncle. We'll take you home soon but first, I need you to show me where the logout point is."

Dolly's voice again, I'm certain of it.

"Log out?" Tears appear on Uncle Carnie's face. "YOU CAN'T LOG OUT!"

"We need your help, Uncle … "

Uncle Carnie rolls to his side, waddles to his feet. He grabs the front of my shirt and begins screaming. "LOG OUT! LOG OUT!" His eyes are bulging out of his face, his breath foul, his tongue covered in sores, his gums oozing pus, his teeth fuzzy and yellow.

Please," I say, "please help us ... help me ... "

I am suddenly overcome with emotion. To think that this algorithmic mishap stands between me and logging out is hard to process.

Picasso's hand comes up, resting on his uncle's back. "Please uncle," he says, "Quantum needs our help."

Uncle Carnie spins around, spins back to me, spins around again. His top hat comes off and he holds it in front of him. "LOG OUT!" he screams into the opening of his hat, "LOG OUT!"

He twists his hat around, smacks the top and an origami star falls out.

"What's that?" I ask.

Picasso picks it up. "It's the logout point."

"But I thought it had to be stationary ... "

"It *is* stationery."

I take the star-shaped piece of paper from Uncle Carnie, examine it. *Stationery.* This was why Frances and I couldn't find the logout point. Naturally, I add it to my inventory list – item 555 (due to the fact I didn't add anything yesterday). It appears in my hand moments later, a small blue indicator floating above it. A banner emerges from the indicator that reads:

Hi, Quantum Hughes. Would you like to log out?

Freedom. Freedom! Freedom!

"Thank you … " I say, my hand hovering over the logout button, my fingers twitching. Then the thought comes to me. "Aiden."

Morning Assassin appears behind my shoulder, lowers his weapon. "Congratulations, Quantum. You found it."

"I'm not finished yet," I tell him, returning the star-shaped stationery to my inventory list. "I need to go back to the hotel."

"Why?"

"I want to thank Dolly. Come on kid," I say to Picasso over my shoulder.

"He's already gone, Quantum," Aiden says.

~*~

There is nothing but debris and amusement park wreckage where Picasso and Uncle Carnie were just standing. A cat-sized rat near the ticket booth rummages through a trashcan; a fiend scratches at his crotch in the shadow of a kiddie ride – this is The Loop. I hear a howl in the distance, and I can't tell if it's human or animal. Doesn't matter now.

"I need to return to the hotel …" I tell him. "One last time."

He nods, knows exactly what I need to do. "I'll go with you."

"Can you do that repopulate-teleport thing?"

"Sure. I not only *can*, I *will*." He rolls his eyes and shakes his head at my confused look. "Grammar," says he. Aiden puts his hand out in front of me. "Touch my hand and we'll be there."

"We really should have done this earlier, instead of taking a taxi."

"Old habits die hard."

"Tell me about it."

I drop my hand onto Aiden's arm and not a second later we're in the lobby of the Mondegreen Hotel. Four of the six morning assassins are sleeping on the sofas. The other two are throwing darts, and Jim the doorman winces every time they miss the target and stick one in the lobby wall.

"Hello, Mr. Hughes," Jim the Doorman says.

"Please, call me Quantum, Jim."

"Hello, Mr. Quantum."

"There 'e is!" Burly the assassin laughs. "We thought you'd never come, mate. Wake up, you slack-jawed load o' poofters!"

Short Irish stretches, yawns, falls off the sofa. He wakes upon impact, struggles to find his weapon.

A pistol appears in Burly's hand and he fires a shot in the ceiling, filling the room with pixilated ceiling-matter. Doorman Jim leaps behind the desk, covering his head with a newspaper. Burly shouts, "Everyone up! The Reapers just called – they're leaving your mum's and are on their way here! STAND TO!"

175

"Why'd you have to bloody do that?" Scotty roars. "I nearly soiled me kilt!" His eyes are bloodshot, his hands form fists in front of him.

"You want a piece o' me, you whinging Scots nancy-boy?" Burly asks, cracking his knuckles.

"Let's 'ave it then, wanker!" Scotty assassin says, his fists coming up.

"Glad to see they're still motivated," I tell Aiden as I make my way to the dining area. "Have them arm up and form a perimeter while I speak to Dolly."

"No problem, Quantum."

"One more thing… " I turn to Morning Assassin, my daily deadly enemy for two subjective years, and not a bad guy once you get to know him. "Thanks for all your help," I say as I put my hand out, "for all you've done."

He walks past my hand and picks me up in a bear hug. "It's been an honor and a pleasure, Quantum. I've really enjoyed working with you."

The Battling Brits shout tasteful encouragement:

"Whyncha just kiss 'im and be done with it?"

"Aren't they just the *dishiest* couple?"

"Don't bonk 'im in the lobby, fer Gossakes!"

"Oi, Jim! You got any vacancies? They look like they could use a room!"

Aiden sets me down, grins at the Brits and gives them the two finger salute. They consider this the height of sophisticated rejoinder and howl their appreciation.

"Seriously, it's been good. If you need me, you know where to find me," and gun in hand, he vanishes.

~*~

"Dolly."

I'm in the dining room at my usual spot, ready for anything. The sky has brightened outside sending in arcs of light, which reflect off the clean plates arranged on each table. I can hear the chef in the kitchen, whistling a show tune. I can hear the Brits bitching at each other in the lobby. I think about going in there and killing them for old time's sake, but decide against it. New days, new ways. No need to revert to the hopeless, kill-crazy animal I once was.

"Quantum."

Dolly stands behind me in a sparkling red dress. Her bob floats above her eyes; her signature make-up tastefully applied – just some eyeliner and deep red lipstick. The diamond necklace I gave her weeks ago sits just above her clavicle. I'd forgotten about the necklace, stolen from a jewelry smuggling operation I happened upon in The Pier. Seeing her with it now only reminds me of how long we've been going at it, whatever *it* may be.

Our history is real no matter what world I exist in.

I hold my arms out to her and she's in them, squeezing me tightly. "I have to go, Dolly," I tell her. "It's time."

"I'm sorry," she says. "I'm sorry for … not helping you escape earlier."

I should be angry but I'm not. There's no way to be angry with Dolly, who is truly the epitome of beautiful, friendly companionship. I understand now that she meant well, that she wasn't trying to hurt me. The moments we spent together – those dance barefoot through my memory as we say our final goodbyes in the dining room where we first met.

She melts against me, tilts her face up and her lips meet mine, soft and warm and full. I say, "Thanks for the help."

"What do you mean?" she asks, her eyes flickering.

"The kid, Picasso. You put him in my life and he led me to the logout point."

A grin, a genuine grin anchored by years of affection spreads across her face. "It was the least I could do."

"I know, but it really helped, Dolly. That's why I've come back here, to thank you, to tell you I'll never forget you and to apologize for all the times … for all the times I've been an idiot."

"CN will have no reason to exist if you aren't here," she says. "You are the only thing keeping this place alive."

My hand rests on the table, holding my weight. "I know," I finally say, "but I'm from a different place entirely and … and I'm practically a skeleton back there. I need some time to fix myself up, to adjust to the real world."

"I wish I could see your world."

Again, her body presses into mine and her hands come to my shoulders.

"It's not all it's cracked up to be, Dolly. Rich versus poor is building steam, or at least it was when I was out there. We have Humandroid androids now, and massive, soulless, profit-grubbing corporations which control every aspect of a person's life, even though

178

most people don't know it. We are an advanced species that may well advance ourselves into extinction if we keep on the way we're going. Still, it's where I'm from, and frankly, I want to go home."

She kisses me again, silencing my tangential maundering. "I want to give you something ... "

We hear shouting outside and the clatter of gunfire. All-out war is approaching.

"Alas!" she says, "The dogs of war doth bark and growl; the rough beasts prowl and seek their prey."

"That quote sounds familiar," I say. "I should know it. Who said it?"

She smiles, taps my nose with her finger. "I just did, silly. Here, I have a gift for you."

A digitized seed appears between us, its form wavering with static. It is oval, about the size of an avocado, rimmed in a blistering light.

"I'm the NVA Seed and this is my origin algorithm. If you access it in any Proxima World, I'll appear."

More gunfire outside. Shouting. Explosions.

"Is that really possible?" I ask, admiring the floating seed.

"Your inventory list is tied to your account; when you return to any Proxima World, you'll still have the same items."

"And I can simply ... access you?"

"Yes, I'll spawn in whatever world you're in. I can also bring Aiden and the six Lobby Assassins ... "

"Aiden?"

"Yes."

"The Battling Brits?"

"Yeah, them too – why not?"

I feel my cheeks stretch as a smile forms. The seed goes to my inventory list, item 556.

"Will you use it then?" she asks. "Will you use the seed?"

"To be honest with you, I haven't thought that far ahead," I say as concussion blows in the windows in the dining room. Bullets spark and spangle off the metal fixtures, divot and crater the sheetrock, and kick debris like confetti into the air.

"Please, Quantum," she says over the sudden commotion, "Don't leave me alone in here forever. Don't forget about me."

The way she says this hurts my heart. "I won't make promises I can't keep, Dolly, but I'll try … "

~*~

A wall blasts open in a gout of fire and bricks and mortar, and Reaper Rollins makes his dramatic entrance. He'd be accompanied by Death Metal theme music if he could arrange for it to happen, and he pauses just long enough to allow us the opportunity to bask in the awesome badness that is him. Both his arms are morphed into large, spiky shark-finned blades with tremendous underslung gun barrels. A gaggle of his lick-spittle posse follow him in, although one is immediately blasted into vapor by an anti-armor rocket from outside, and the others whirl, crouch and return fire. The firing outside slackens for a moment, and the cat-calls and raucous laughter drift in with the gun smoke.

"Ooh! That's gonna leave a mark in the morning!"

"Bet that made the big la-de-dah poofter poo in his tutu!"

"Oi, Rollins – me ol' Gran and 'er Colecovison are tougher than you lot with this ProximaTech!"

"You load o' wankers are as soft as shite!"

"*Mon canard est un feu,* eh mate?"

Rollins' bruxism is audible even over the firing and explosions.

"How many of our guys are left?" I ask Dolly.

"Aiden, and four of the Lobby Boys. And Jim and the chef – they're out there too; they wanted to help." she says, as she assumes a defensive martial arts posture.

"You don't have to fight them with me … "

"You shouldn't fight them at all," she says. "You should let me handle this. Log out before they—"

A solid wall of fire erupts from Rollins' two mutant hacks. Before I can react, Dolly steps in front of me, shielding me from the blast. It cascades over her, strips her substance from her in streamers of energy, melting her away like a snowman at the gates of Hell. She stands there, an incandescent angel of fire as Rollins bellows with laughter. I scream in wordless rage and move to return fire when Rollins' fire winks out, and suddenly she's

181

Johnny Storm, then T-1000, then Dolly again. She turns to me and her eyes flash orange, lit from within by some terrible furnace.

Rollins fires again and this time his blast never touches her; it stops dead, inches away in defiance of all the laws of physics.

"You can do that?" I ask.

"Log out, Quantum, go NOW!"

I've waited years for this moment; dreamt about it, fantasized about it, lusted after it and suddenly I don't want to do it; suddenly I don't want to leave Dolly.

"Now, Quantum, please! I don't want you to see this!" She's suddenly larger, darker, frightening, and the light in the room streams into her like matter into a black hole. Rollins shrieks like a sissy in sheer, unadulterated, sphincter-loosening terror.

I press the logout button and for the first time in eight years, I hear the logout tone.

~*~

Air enters my lungs; it's warm, moist, tastes of nothing. I'm on my back, floating. I wait for the feedback, and I wait, and I wait, and I wait. Instead, a quiet, gentle, friendly voice materializes between my ears.

Welcome back, Quantum Hughes. You are in an Individual Life Support Tank at the TransProxima Insurance Trust Digital Coma Long-Term Care Facility located in Cincinnati, Ohio. Today is Thursday, May twenty-third, two thousand fifty-eight. The current time is ten forty-seven PM and thirty-eight seconds.

The automatic extraction and revival will begin momentarily. Please do not be alarmed. We are about to engage ... The Nozzle. Please do not move while The Nozzle is engaging. Moving will disrupt calibration of ... The Nozzle. Please wait while we calibrate ... The Nozzle. Please do not look away from ... The Nozzle. The Nozzle is now calibrating. The Nozzle is still calibrating. The Nozzle has completed calibration. Thank you.

Medical personnel have been summoned and will assist you momentarily. Please relax and remain stationary. Please do not be alarmed as we remove your respirator and Neuronic Vision Visor.

I couldn't move if I wanted to.

I wiggle my fingers and toes, try to lift my arms and legs – no joy. Soft mechanical fingers remove my breathing tube, disconnect my NV Visor.

Then it hits me like a brick in the back of the noggin – *I'm OUT!* I suck in another lungful of filtered industrial medical facility air and it's *wonderful!* Actual photons reflected from actual objects in the actual world actually enter my eyes and are actually processed by my visual cortex – *marvelous!*

Various whirrings and stirrings and clinkings and clankings are going on around me as the ArachnaMed does its extraction and recovery thing. My vision blurs, sharpens, blurs again. I blink rapidly, try to get hold of myself, blink again. The world around me regains its sharpness as my eyes adjust.

Four men in scrubs and lab coats wheel a gurney into my peripheral vision. I turn my head and open my mouth to speak, but all I manage to produce is a dry croaking.

"Yeah, it's him. Dive vat data plaque states SAMUEL BECKETT; plaque's chip confirms QUANTUM HUGHES," the first guy says. He's crew-cut, hard-eyed, lantern-jawed. Somehow, he doesn't fit my idea of what a medical tech should look like, but who am I to judge? There isn't a sea-going crustaceous bi-valve on the planet that's happier than yours truly right about now.

I blink and my eyes blur and refocus. Second guy is big, black, bulky, shaved head, soul patch. He doesn't look very med tech-y either. He looks me in the eye and asks, "Quantum Hughes?"

"Yeah ... " I manage to whisper. "Yeah ... "

He smiles, ducks his head slightly, puts his finger to his ear, "Break, break – Control, this is Charlie-one. We have the subject; identity confirmed ... Roger that, we got him. Extracting now; estimate complete in ten mike, will advise."

He turns back to me and says, "Rollins sends his regards."

Suddenly, I'm not so happy. I do what struggling I can, but I'm still attached to the mechanical exoframe that exercised my limbs. My efforts barely ripple the surface of the semi-fluid vat gel. "Help!" I gasp to the SpiderDoc above me. "Help!" I try again.

Guy number three has dark hair in a *Pulp Fiction* ponytail and an *evil Spock* goatee. He pops the cover off of some piece of vat equipment, examines it for a moment and jacks in with a handheld device.

"C'mon, McAfee, quickly! We need to move!" Number Two hisses.

Number Three puts down the handheld, straightens up and says, "Tell you what – you go ahead and spoof the alarms and execute an emergency disconnect and I'll stand there and give you shit ... No? Then shut yer hole and let me do my job!"

"Excuse me, gentlemen. This is a restricted area and you're not allow ... " the Humandroid nurse begins, just as Number Four shoots him twice in the chest and once in the head. Alarms blare. Red lights strobe and a mechanical voice sounds off. "INTRUDER ALERT! INTRUDER ALERT! WEAPONS FIRE BAY FIVE, BLOCK SEVEN, UNIT TWO-ONE!"

"IDIOT! IDIOT!" Number Two roars. "Norton! You worthless, trigger-happy fu … " He gets hold of himself. "Dammit! Secure the entrance and hold 'em off. Kapersky, you go secure our exit. GO!"

I never got a good look at Number Four, Norton, as he sprints off in the direction the Humandroid nurse came from. Kapersky, Number One, charges back the way they came.

Finger to the ear, Number Two says, "Break, Break – Control this is Charlie-one. We've been blown; Charlie-four engaged 'droid staff and triggered alarms." He waits, listens. "Roger that, but contract states he's worth more alive; will attempt to extract, will advise."

Worth more alive?

"Alrighty, then," Number Two says to Number Three. "Quick and dirty," as he pulls a compact machine pistol from underneath the gurney and attempts to look in all directions at the same time. Number Three climbs up into the vat, straddles me and starts slicing straps, tubes, wires and leads with a chainknife.

Gunfire erupts from both directions, interspersed with the *buzz-snap* of PHASRs set to stun.

I float free and Number Three drops his chainknife into the vat.

"He's clear!" Number Three shouts, puts his arms under me and tries to lift me out. I flop like a boneless chicken in the button man's clutches. I'm slippery with vat gel, and I feel my spine twist and pop as he loses his grip, drops me. He tries again and really jacks up my spine before he lets go the second time and I slide back onto the exoframe.

"Hurry!" Number Two curses at his counterpart, fires several short bursts from his weapon, curses again. "Change of plan! Do him, get out of there and let's go!"

Number Three puts his hand on my face and pushes it under the surface. Terror surges through me and clutches me in its grip; pink-tinged vat gel stings my eyes and I try to blink it out. My finger moves but my inventory list won't come up. The goon is going to drown me like a kitten, and there's nothing I can do.

I hear the muffled thudding of Number Two's machine pistol; all I can think of is Dolly waiting in vain for me to return; waiting for as long as the Proxima Galaxy endures, waiting until the heat death of the universe.

I'm so sorry, Dolly!

A brilliant violet flash lights up my world.

Number Three's hand slides off my face and I surface, gasp in huge plumes of air. He's been PHASR stunned, and flops across my body, face-down. I know I don't have a whole lot of time before he shakes it off, but now that I'm free of the exoframe I can move some; I can move enough…

I walk my fingers up over the back of his neck.

I get a good grip on his *I'm so cool* ponytail and focus everything I got on pushing his face into the gel, holding it there. He never twitches.

The bubbling and sputtering eventually stops, but I keep his face in the gel, just to be sure.

I have time to consider my position as I semi-float in the vat with Number Three's ponytail still in my fist. I'm back in the world, and it's the bee's knees, the cat's meow; it's ace, it's killer, it's top shelf – yes indeedy. However, I'm in pain, actual pain, and it troughs and crests through my body. The novelty's long since worn off, and I'm ready for it to quit. The intruder alarm is still bleating in my skull, and it's not helping the headache I've got going on that would cripple a lesser man. Plus, I'm hungry – really hungry. A stack of pancakes, extra butter, crispy fried bacon, two eggs over easy, three slices of toast and a cold one would go a long way right about now.

And I wish Dolly could bring it to me.

The alarm and the red strobes cut off, and the house lights come up bright, a bright that burns into my brain, even with my eyes closed. Loud voices shout back and forth: "Clear!" and "Clear!" and "One hostile down over here!" and "Clear!"

A man with a gun – big gun – reaches over the edge of the vat and feels Number Three's neck for a pulse, then feels for mine. He puts his finger to his ear. "Hughes is still alive, second hostile down. Say again, Hughes is alive, second hostile down."

Epilogue

June 20th 2058.

A wheelchair – how retro. They offered me a powered exoskeleton that would let me walk immediately, engage in *daily activities of living* as they euphemistically put it, and perform my physical therapy all at the same time.

No. Thank. You.

Granted, it's a powered AI wheelchair and I steer it with finger flicks when some Humandroid attendant isn't pushing, but still it's better than walking around like a Series 800 Model 101. But despite the pain, despite the injuries, despite the physical limitations, I've never felt better, I've never felt more alive.

Freedom is the smell of grass in the morning. Freedom is the sound of crickets chirping in the evening. Freedom is the ability to wake up and fall back to sleep; to awaken without worrying about where the next ambush will be, wondering who's going to try to kill you *this* time.

Freedom is color, rich, vibrant color.

True – I'm still having problems adjusting to color. True – keeping my eyes open during the botched extraction has distorted my vision, something that will also require surgery or a pair of good Leaks, which apparently have improved while I was stuck in The Loop. Still, *freedom is color*.

The parade of humanity goes past my window every day, even though *humanity* is mostly just the pair of Humandroids who manage the hospital's landscaping. Watching them gives me a sense of delight greater than sex, drugs, rock 'n' roll, money, or anything else that tickles the "ol dopamine receptors. I'm in constant-smile mode, no matter how painful things are or how tired I am of being fed through a tube.

It's been said before and I'll say it again: life is a beautiful thing.

A nurse peeks in. "You have a visitor, Quantum," she says.

"Who is it this time? Cop, lawyer, insurance adjuster?"

"A young lady."

Frances Euphoria.

I know it's her without the nurse having to say another word. Frances has been in D.C. dealing with the Federal Bureau of Investigation and Intelligence Gathering's inquiry into the attempted assault and kidnapping of Mrs. Hughes' eldest unmarried son by alleged Industrial Espionage Operatives, and not Reapers – who don't exist according to the F-BIIG. Two of the four not-Reapers survived and lawyered up immediately.

Still, an investigation is probably imminent.

"Send her in."

This is the first time Frances and I will meet in the real world, and I'm a little nervous about it. I raise my hand to brush my hair out of my eyes, and the IV line pulls and I remember I don't have long hair in the real world; nothing to sweep aside. My hands come down and I smooth the front of my stylish hospital bathrobe.

Frances enters, and she looks nothing like her avatar. She has dark brown eyes and short black hair cut in a military high-and-tight. She's thin, but still fills her blouse nicely, if you know what I mean, and she holds herself in an assertive, no BS manner. I imagine that I don't look much like my avatar, either. Eight years in the vat have probably not added a beach-boy tan or given me a gym-rat physique, and really I don't want to know just how much ground I've lost. Seeing my arms and legs is bad enough; a mirror would probably finish me.

Frances closes the door, sits in front of me and immediately turns on the waterworks.

"Really? Am I that bad?"

"No, no … it's not that. I just can't believe I'm seeing you alive," she says. "It still … gets to me."

"Not much to look at." I run my hand across my shaved head, pinch my earlobe.

"You'll gain color again and weight, regain muscle tone," she assures me.

"Yeah, in that order."

"So, do you remember me now?" she asks.

"Should I? What do you mean?"

"We never talked about why I came for you in The Loop."

"That's what you do, isn't it?"

"It is, but … " She smiles through her tears. "You're the one who *gave* me this job."

"Me?"

She nods. "I was trapped in a Proxima World called Arrakis, a desert planet taken from the *Dune* series. You rescued me, back in 2049, when I was sixteen years old. At the time, you and your partner, Strata Godsick, had just gotten federal funding from the FCG to perform your first rescue. *I was that rescue.*"

"And I hired you?"

"No, but you inspired me to join as soon as I turned eighteen, after hearing that you yourself were trapped in an unknown Proxima World yourself."

My eyes dart to the window, where I catch an actual breeze rustling through the trees. Knowing that it isn't digital, that it isn't some clever algorithm, makes me incredibly grateful, grateful for Frances for freeing me. "Thank you," I say, "Thank you for coming after me even though I was basically forgotten."

"It was an honor and a privilege, Quantum. I'd gladly do it again," she says.

Silence settles in the air between us. Someone pushes a gurney through the hallway outside of the door, its wheels loud and squeaky. The Rehab Facility smells of disinfectant, plastic, ozone.

Frances is the first to speak. "I have a personal favor to ask of you."

"Go on."

"I wanted to ask you if you're willing to join the Dream Team once you recover. After all, you are one of its founders ..."

I almost laugh at her proposition. There is *no way* I'm going to subject myself to a VE dreamworld again, even if it's essentially the same as dreaming. *Even if Dolly's there...*

"You've got to be kidding me," I finally tell her.

"But Quantum ... " she bites her lip. "There are others like me, like you, people who are trapped and whom the Reapers are killing for profit. Developers and regular users."

"The Reapers." Just saying the word puts a bad taste in my mouth.

"We'd be able to fight them as a team," she says, "and now that you're out here, we'll get you enhanced weapons for your next visit."

"How enhanced?" I'm not thinking of re-upping, I'm just idly curious, that's all. Just curious.

"We have a coder and a former military cyber-warfare operative on our team responsible for weapons development. They've reverse engineered most of the new mutant hacks the Reapers use, and have developed several really nasty ones that the Reapers don't have. These are game-changers; these are war-winners." She becomes fiercely intense, "We can take the fight to them, make them fight on our terms, put them on the defensive."

"That's great and all, Frances, but there is no way I'm going back into the Proxima Galaxy. Not even for … "

I think of Dolly, her bob haircut, her ruby red lips, our relationship that spanned eight years.

"Even for what?"

"Nothing."

She stands, runs her hands along her outfit, which is black, collarless, and cut in a military style. "Think about it, will you? I have to get going."

"I will, but I can tell you now that the answer will still be no." I look back out the window. Never mind virtual reality – actual reality is where it's at, pussycat.

That's why, Frances, that's why.

She bends forward and kisses me on the cheek. "It was nice seeing you, seeing that you are recovering."

"Thanks for all you've done," I say, looking her eye to eye.

"Thank you as well, Quantum."

Frances is almost at the door when I ask, "Whatever happened to my partner, the one who started the Dream Team with me? You never told me about him."

"You still don't know, do you?"

"No," I admit. 'my memory has been … fuzzy."

"Your former partner, Strata Godsick, is the one who started the Revenue Corporation. He is the leader of the Reapers."

My throat tightens. "Strata Godsick?"

Images materialize in my mind's eye at the sound of his name. I can see Godsick now in his Dream Team uniform, can see us shaking hands, can see the Reaper skull mask, can see Rollins pointing his nightmare weapons at me, can feel the bleachies grabbing at my legs.

"He's the one who started the Reapers?"

"Yes, he's the head of their murder guild."

"He put a hit out on me … "

"Yes," Frances says, "and he has killed plenty of others. We calculate he's been directly or indirectly responsible for the death of more than five hundred people. These are just the confirmed deaths – there may be two or three times as many more that we can't confirm. And that doesn't take into account the users he's enslaved."

"The bleached people."

"Yes," she says.

193

"C'mere." I reach my out, with the arm that doesn't have all the tubes in it.

She takes my hand, gently squeezes my arm, waits, says nothing.

I look up at her and muster the biggest smile I can possibly muster. "I'll do it. I'll come back. Somebody needs to stop these cyber-Nazis, these bullies, these corporate greed-heads. So yeah, I'll do it. I'm in. Where do I sign up?"

"You will?" She mostly contains her excitement, mostly. But there is a happy dance just below the surface that's going to bubble out as soon as she's alone.

"But first … "

"Yes! Anything!"

"But first, I want to get better, and then I want you to take me out for a beer and some pancakes. I'm sick of being fed through a tube."

She laughs. "Anything you want, Quantum, anything."

Outside the sun shines brightly and birds spiral to heights unknown. The clouds have all but disappeared; the day is clear, calm. Everyone deserves to see this; everyone deserves to bear witness to a beautiful summer day in the real world. No one deserves to be trapped in a VE dreamworld, stripped of their hope and humanity, their deaths or entrapment used to increase the profit margin of some evil corporate entity.

A fire burns in my belly. *I will recover and then I will come for you, Strata Godsick.* I will defeat you, here and in the Proxima Galaxy.

The End

Back of the Book Shit

Dear Reader,

The Feedback Loop was modeled off a number of things, most notably a movie called Groundhog Day, the writing style of Charles Bukowski, Pulp Fiction, two manga/anime series called Sword Art Online and Tokyo Ghoul (can be viewed for free at kissanime.com), the science fiction book *Ready Player One* and the comic book series, Sin City. The formation of the Proxima World was based on an article I read in *The New Yorker* called "World without End," by Raffi Khatchadourian. I wanted to blend all these things into Cyber Noir or The Loop, and place a character inside it who couldn't log out.

Lately, I've been casting movie and television actors in my head to better write characters. Quantum Hughes is Michael Pitt, Frances Euphoria is Charlize Theron (or Scarlett Johansson on some days), Morning Assassin is Adam Driver, Dolly is Laura Prepon with the voice of Yael Stone (both from the show *Orange is the New Black*.)

The Feedback Loop Series takes place twenty-five years before my other science-fiction series, Life is a Beautiful Thing. For readers of both series, you've likely noticed that The Feedback Loop is tame compared to my other series. For those who haven't checked out Life is a Beautiful Thing, I suggest getting it on Amazon here or signing up for my reader's group and getting the first two books for free as it is a wild ride. I should warn you though – it is vulgar, insane, violent, cutting-edge, bizarre and everything in between.

More on the Feedback Loop.

This book was written over the month of May 2015. I prepped for a month beforehand, taking notes, working on the story arc and finalizing the VE dreamworld concepts. Originally, Quantum Hughes was supposed to be in love with Frances Euphoria, but as the book developed, the time he spent with Dolly became more and more important, even though it doesn't take a center role in the story until the middle-end.

Quantum's speech pattern, especially some of the phrases he uses, was borrowed from lists I found detailing idioms and other unique verbs used predominantly in the 1940s and 50s. I tried to use these types of words and phrases as much as I could, as I wanted to show that he had picked up these colloquialisms in The Loop and had since appropriated them. Dolly also benefited from my idiom research. This is pointed out once or twice in the manuscript by Frances (calling Quantum out), but I wanted to keep the focus more on the action rather than his antiquated expressions.

I suppose I like exploring these concepts, the future of relationships if you will. Quantum's time with Dolly the NVA Seed is an example of this in The Feedback Loop. In my other series, Meme's relationship with a Humandroid named Yeshi also explores this futuristic dilemma. It is an interesting thing to think about, especially as our dependency on technology progresses. Maybe I'll be alive long enough to see the first human/A.I. relationships.

Thanks to my girlfriend, Sor Ganbold, for reading an early draft while riding on an old Soviet train and encouraging me further. Also, a special pollute-filled thanks goes out to Ben for helping me craft the product description and Dale for reading an early version of said product description onboard a ship (not the Titanic). I am a one-man band at times, drumming for nobody but the voices in my head. I appreciate those who've stumbled upon me and encourage me further. The biggest thanks possible goes out to Kay in Scotland, who advised me on the difference between stationary and stationery (!), and whose keen eye greatly improved the novel.

Thanks as large as Rollins" muscles go out to my editor, George C. Hopkins, for his beautiful work on this piece. This book is littered with more obscure movie and literature references than a sane man could list here and most were suggested by George. Further, he greatly improved the style of the manuscript and greatly inspired my edit of the second book in the series, Steampunk is Dead. If you've enjoyed the read and ever find yourself in Goose Country, buy this man a beer or three.

Also, if you caught the word phorusrhacid you may want a better explanation on the fascinating terror birds. Look no further than an email George recently sent me on the troubled species:

"Everybody should care about Phorusrhacidae, a 10 foot tall, razor-sharp eagle-beaked apex predator capable of speeds up to 30MPH, with feet equipped with Velociraptor claws! Especially the de-extincted ones that were illicitly hatched by the same type of dumbass that keeps a Bengal Tiger in a trailer park, and then released into the wild by these same dumbasses when they got too expensive to feed and kept eating their pitbulls.

The smaller species of phorusrhacidae (about 3 - 4 foot tall) make excellent guardians for geese, but you have to raise them together as hatchlings so the phorusrhacidae imprint on the geese, think of themselves as geese and see the geese as family and not food.

Rhacids are hell on the squirrels, rats and mice, foxes, raccoons, armadillos, feral dogs and cats, and bobcats. They'll pick up the feral piglets, and have a NorK/SouK standoff type of understanding with the adult feral hogs.

They're not too crazy about the skunks after getting sprayed the first time, and they make the goats nervous even though they think of the goats as especially ungainly, unfeathered, four-legged geese.

The UPS, USPS, and FedEx delivery drivers are only supposed to drop off at the outer perimeter fence in the drop-off box SPECIALLY PROVIDED for that purpose, especially after that one time a UPS driver that wasn't the regular gal was stuck inside her truck for 18 hours after she ignored the 'Beware of Terror Birds, Trespassers Will Be EATEN' and 'DO NOT ENTER! Biosecurity Enforcement Area! Help Keep Our Flock Healthy. DO NOT ENTER!' signs and came inside the outer perimeter fence. The combined flock swarmed the truck and the Rhacids flattened her tires."

TLDR – don't screw around with Terror Birds, be they extinct, de-extincted or on their way to extinction.

In unrelated news:

Steampunk is Dead – aka Book Two in the Feedback Loop Series – is available here on Amazon. The book introduces a new world for Quantum and company to explore, and **there is a sample of the book at the back of this book.**

Review me. Independent authors thrive on reviews, as they provide encouragement and help get our books in the hands of other readers.

If you'd like to get started on the Life is a Beautiful Thing Series I mentioned earlier, sign up for my reader's group to receive a free three book box set. **I'll even throw in a free copy of Steampunk is Dead.** This should get you adequately started on the series. Book Three and Four in the series are out now. You can also sign up for my reader's group at www.harmoncooper.com

Thanks for taking the time to read this and supporting independent authors. Your reviews and patronage go a long way. **Review, review, review,** and I'll keep pecking away at this fun series.

Until we meet again on a page of ink or paper,

Harmon Cooper, July 2015

Writer.harmoncooper@gmail.com

Steampunk is Dead -- the exciting sequel to The Feedback Loop.

Adjusting to the real world isn't exactly easy for Quantum Hughes. Instead of focusing on his recovery, he takes an assignment alongside Frances Euphoria to a virtual entertainment dreamworld called Steam, in search of a Proxima Developer. True to his nature, Quantum acts out of turn, causing the entire world to turn against him. This gives him two options: return to The Loop for help, or try and hold his own. There is also the problem of the Reapers, who have appeared in Steam ready to hunt him down or worse, kill him.

The real world, The Loop, Steam -- three worlds with their own rules, their own enemies.

The thin line between dream and reality is pixilated.

You can read chapter one of Steampunk is Dead on the following page.

Steampunk is Dead (sample)

The Feedback Loop BOOK TWO

Harmon Cooper

Edited by George C. Hopkins

Chapter One

I try in vain to access my inventory list. My finger taps against thin air, waiting for my inventory list to appear. *Come on you bastard...*

Another kick to the stomach reminds me of where I am, lying in a dirty, greasy, urine-soaked alley, watching the stars and planets whirl about in my own private planetarium and feeling genuine, full-body pain the likes of which I haven't felt in years. Blood on my lips, blood on my chin, blood on the pavement. The fight already lost, the white flag tattered.

"Come on," I say tapping my finger in the air. "Come on ... "

Another kick reminds me of how real the *real* world is, how stupid I must look trying to access my inventory list. From trouble boys and trigger men to snowed up shitbirds – the story of my life.

Pathetic, Quantum.

My eyes blur as I take in the man's stompers, oversized things that make him look like a toddler in his dad's sneakers.

"Ya got something else to say, ya bastid?" my assailant asks. He is East Coast to the core – that accent we've come to love and despise coupled with muscles and grease. No ducktail, but definitely slicked back. The type of palooka I shouldn't have messed with, the type of jasper who gets high off pollutes and assaults a feeble guy like me, a man with a cane. Maybe I should have opted for cyborg replacements or an exoskeletal suit. What can I say? A man has his convictions.

A kick to my thigh this time.

"C'mon – is that all you got? My sistuh hits hahduh than you! Stand up, ya pussy! Fight me like a man!"

"Leave him alone, Jimmy, he ain't shit."

You are not in The Loop.

The reminder has little or no effect. Still trying to access my list, still trying to choose a weapon – anything – to handle the wise guy who's kicking me like I'm a recalcitrant Harley. What I wouldn't give to access my vintage stag-handled Bowie knife – item 33 – and slice him into greaser jerky, hang his carcass up to dry. What I wouldn't give to activate my advanced abilities bar, spring into the air and land behind him and crack the back of his neck over my shoulder. Send Mr. Tough guy to the morgue before he can utter another word. Make sure the only thing he can do for the next week is eat out of a tube.

I suppose the name of the game is maim, even in the real world. Another kick and I spit blood. Real blood, my blood, no digital sap allowed.

"Youah wimpy and weak!" The man bends over and socks me in the face. "Ya heah me? *Weak!*"

If only we could have met somewhere else...

A final kiss from his big boot sends a sharp pain ballooning through my body. My finger comes up to access my inventory list and I hear laughter.

"Let's get out of heah, Jimmy," the man's friend says as a police siren knifes the air. "This guy's a real freak."

Welcome to the real world, Quantum.

205

~*~

"State your name for the record please, this Field Interview is being recorded." the police officer says. The walls of the alley strobe *red-blue-blue-red; red-blue-blue-red* with sufficient intensity to induce an epileptic seizure. I sit with my back against a dumpster, clutch my cane, and try to make sense of what's just gone down.

"Quantum Hughes," I mumble.

His pupils dilate and completely occlude the iris as he scans me – okay, this one's not human, then. No, he's part of a new Humandroid Police Program, something I would not have believed eight years ago, when I first got stuck in The Loop. There were Humandroids before I got trapped in The Loop, but they weren't as advanced as they are now. Definitely not advanced enough for law enforcement. Now here's *Homo Machina Lex Congendi Officiariis,* genuine *Mechanica Porcum Americanus* if you will, in the artificial flesh. Next it'll be ED-209s on every street corner. Who'd have thought it'd come to this? Mechanical fuzz? Goodbye civil liberties and our rapidly eroding constitutional guarantees.

"Look, RoboCop, I want to speak to a real person," I say, ignoring the pain in my jaw every time I flap my gums.

"You require medical treatment," the Humandroid tells me. "You have a fractured rib and cranio-facial injuries indicative of potential traumatic brain injury."

"Who are you? Dr. McCoy? Dr. Spock? Dr. Seuss? How do you know?" I ask, as the planet rotates around me.

"I've scanned your vitals twice now."

"Dammit droid, I want to speak to someone who can help me find the scum who did this to me."

"I understand, Mr. Hughes."

"Quantum, call me Quantum, and quit giving me the third degree!"

"I understand, Mr. Quantum. A human police officer is on the way. In the meantime, please tell me what happened in your own words."

"You want to know what happened?" I look up at the Humandroid. If I hadn't seen his pupils dilate, I would have assumed he was as human as me.

"Please, in detail. The video from the surveillance equipment in this alley will help us to positively identify the alleged perpetrators."

"Surveillance equipment? Wait a minute – *alleged* perpetrators?"

"Yes sir. Unless and until the individuals in question are apprehended, processed, tried, and convicted they are the *alleged* perpetrators. In accordance with the Watch Our Own People Act of 2036, surveillance equipment has been installed in all public spaces, particularly those where statistical probability indicates criminal activity is likely to transpire."

I sigh. "Listen, droid ... "

His voice goes flat and not-quite-menacing, "Mr. Hughes, my official designation is Mark9 Patrol Officer, Unit 2315. You may address me by some variation thereof. Do *not* address me as *droid* again. This is your first, last, and only warning."

"Mark9 Patrol Officer? Do you know my buddy Mark8? He and I go way back … " I say with a blood dappled grin. I've been back in the real world for nearly a month now – giving droids hell is something I've come to enjoy.

"Very humorous, Mr. Quantum. I'll be sure to recount it to the other Mark9s at the precinct who will without doubt enjoy it as much as I have. Now then Mr. Quantum, in detail, what happened?"

"All right, Marky Mark all right. So I stepped into the bar … "

"Paddy's Pub."

"Sure, whatever. Anyways, I sit down and have a beer. Then I have another beer. Then I have another, 'nother beer."

"Three beers."

"You got a calculator app, too? Listen, Ro-Man, I wasn't going over the edge with the rams or anything – got it? I was just having a few cold ones. Nothing wrong with that. This is still a free-ish country, dammit."

"Indeed sir. Is this your blood on the ground here?"

"Well, let's see, Marlowe. That's the spot I was lying in when you showed up, I'm the only one here that's bleeding. So yeah, there's a *statistical probability* that it's my blood." I can talk like a tight-ass too.

"Yes, sir. Is this your blood; please answer *yes* or *no*."

"Yes, yes – it's my blood. What, are you the Blood Police? You gonna charge me with littering for getting my blood all over this nice clean alley?

He takes a small applicator out of a pouch on his belt, delicately swabs it in the blood – *my* blood, holds the applicator in thumb and pointer finger and dilates his pupils again as he reads it."

My eyes narrow. "What's the big idea?"

The Humandroid officer flatly states, "Adjusting for your weight, stomach contents, and metabolic rate, your blood alcohol concentration in parts per million indicates you have consumed more than three beers. You are well above the legal limit, sir."

"Oh, you're frickin' *CSI Baltimore* now? Well, there's nothing wrong with that is there? I'm not operating an aeros, ground vehicle, or heavy equipment; I'm not on a hoverboard, Imperial speeder bike or unicycle. I don't even have a hayburner or nothing."

He produces a small Ziploc bag, places the swab inside, and secures the bag in his bat-utility belt. "Very well, Mr. Quantum. Do tell me what happened in Paddy's Pub."

"Okay, so maybe I had six beers. The point is, I saw these two goons across the bar looking at me funny, gowed-up on pollutes."

"Describe the men."

"Buff, slicked back hair, dangly earrings, fake tan, maybe Italian, Puerto Rican, Greek, Martian, Joey from *Friends* – who knows. I got no idea what the filth were doing here in Baltimore."

"And were they drinking?"

"Are you listening to me? They were using pollutes."

Pollutes are the name for designer inhalants dispensed by pollution masks, which were developed in the 2040s. They've become quite popular in the eight years I was marooned in The Loop, although personally I don't see what all the fuss is about. Who wants to sit around like an aardvark with a rhinovirus snuffling in designer gasses when you can marinate your brain cells in good 'ol EtOH like God intended? What the hell is wrong with people these days anyway? I'm not saying eel juice is for everyone, but it beats sitting around in neo-plague masks sucking down dope.

"So the two men were using pollutes?" the Humandroid asks.

"Do I need to spell it out for you?"

"And then what happened?"

"One of them took off his mask and asked me if I was looking at him funny."

"And how did you reply?"

"I don't remember."

"What do you remember?"

I scowled at the droid, but the change in my facial expression didn't seem to register with him. "I remember one of them asking if I'd like to take it outside. Well, I obliged, and I got one good one in with my cane before he overpowered me."

"I see. So you state that you committed the initial assault, and the subsequent physical injuries you received were a direct result of that individual acting in lawful self-defense. Does that accurately describe what happened?" he asks.

"I... wait, what?" My eyes move from the officer's perfectly sculpted face to a streetlamp in the distance. *Don't give yourself away, Quantum.*

"Does that accurately describe what happened?"

"I don't remember."

This is turning not good way too fast. I stand, wobbly, but at least I'm on my feet. Leaning my weight on my aluminum cane helps some, but not much. I'm not the biggest fan of my new walking buddy, but it's better than a wheelchair. "Look, Mark9 Patrol Officer Unit 2315, Can we just forget about the whole thing? I've got to get going."

"Do you desire to make an official statement?"

"No, I'd like to go back to my hotel."

"I'll escort you, Mr. Hughes."

"Quantum, call me Quantum."

~*~

The hotel I'm staying at in Baltimore isn't far from the gin mill, just a couple of blocks. It's an elaborate affair, with a half-donut driveway and an expansive lobby. Too much room for me; I prefer something a little cozier, something a little more disheveled, something like The Mondegreen Hotel in The Loop.

"You should receive medical attention," Mark9 Patrol Officer suggests once we arrive at the hotel. "I can summon emergency services if you desire."

I shake my head. "No meat wagons. I've seen enough sawbones over the last month to last me a lifetime. I've been poked, prodded, picked over and examined ..."

"So your life chip data states," he says.

"Life chip data?" The bottom drops out of my stomach. "I didn't authorize a ... a damn life chip!"

"It was likely inserted it during one of your surgical procedures, as lifechip evasion is a federal offense. The life chip allows the Federal Corporate Government to better administer to its citizens' needs. Yours indicates that you've recently had corrective spinal surgery and that you were in a digital coma for eight years."

I tap the tip of my cane against the polished marble floor. A looker walks by with a pair of getaway sticks worthy of a pinup mag. I shoot her a toothy grin and she ignores me. My thoughts return to the fact that I've been chipped like a shelter puppy – now I'm traceable, trackable, watchable and blackmailable.

Thanks a lot, Frances Euphoria. She's the one who signed off on my medical procedures. My fists tighten as I turn away from the droid.

"If I have a life chip," I say through gritted teeth, "why did you ask me my name back there?"

"It is standard procedure to ask a citizen their name during a field interview. It helps to establish a friendlier officer-citizen interaction. Studies have shown that an estimated–"

"Whatever, copper, I've got it from here."

I'm in the elevator a minute later, heading to my floor. Fuming doesn't begin to describe my disposition. In the past thirty minutes, I've had my ass royally handed to me and been told that there is now a CPU called a life chip installed in my head that can be used for God-knows-what. This on top of the fact that I have to give witness testimony tomorrow has my blood boiling.

As soon as I'm in my hotel room I pick up the phone and call the number Frances Euphoria gave me.

"Dammit, Frances," I say instead of hello.

"Quantum?" she chuckles to herself. "Ah that's right; you're calling on a landline. I haven't received a call on a landline in ages."

"Did you know that a life chip was installed in my head?"

"Yes," she says, yawning. "Why?"

"I told you I didn't want one! I just got my ass kicked and the droid police officer tells me all these things about me based solely on the data of my life chip. It gave me the creeps."

"Ass kicked? Are you all right?"

"I'm fine. The life chip–"

"Everyone in America has a life chip," she says. "It's federal law. I was planning on showing you how to use it tomorrow, after your witness testimony."

"So it's active?"

"Your life chip *is* active, but it can't connect to iNet or anything."

"iNet?" I mouth the words again. "Oh, yeah, internet inside my eyelids, the thing that everyone uses. Great, that's the last thing I need..."

"It's quite useful, much more convenient than Wi-Fi. Don't act like you haven't seen people using it before. You've been out of the recovery ward for a week now."

"I was at my dad's place; he doesn't use this shit."

"Yes, he does – everyone has one."

The thought of my dad reminded me why I was drinking at the dive bar in the first place. My mom died two weeks before I logged out of The Loop. The woman who had named me and raised me and cared for me was gone. I couldn't help but feel bitter about it. *Two weeks before I woke up.*

As Frances tells me about tomorrow's plans, my eyes settle on the Proxima VE rig set up in the room. There's an NV visor and even a reclining haptic chair.

"I have to go Frances," I say.

"Do you want me to come over or not? I'm about twenty minutes away, at the office."

"Are you sleeping there now?"

"No, I'm talking to you using nineteenth century technology now. I'm coming over, Quantum. Stay put."

"Well if you do, bring some first-aid supplies and a bottle of Jack."

~*~

I know better than to put the Neuronal Visualization Visor on. I haven't been to a Proxima World since I finally logged out, but here I am, relaxing in the haptic chair and ready to visit The Loop. As soon as the visor comes over my eyes I hear a soft dinging sound created by Brian Eno, signaling the network is ready to take me.

"What are you doing?" I ask aloud.

Of course no one answers. Who would answer?

"I'm coming Dolly, I'm coming back for you."

Dolly, the NVA Seed with whom I had a relationship with for damn near a decade – I've thought about her every day since returning to the real world, the world that just treated me to a good ol' fashioned, East Coast-style "Welcome Back, Moron!" ass-kicking, now with thirty percent more bruises and contusions. Despite that, I'd love to somehow show her this world, to take her on a stroll through a park, hold her hand, feed some fat pigeons, catch a flick afterwards. Normal things.

Our time together comes to me in a series of flashes. Funny how memories do that. Breaking into the room next to mine to watch old movies, the hours we spent lying on my bed listening to the storm outside, the time she tried to kill me, the time she saved me, the time she morphed into something otherworldly once the Reapers arrived.

I can see her now, standing in front of me in a tight red dress, her hair in a bob, her lips crimson, chewing gum as she curls into my lap, relaxes into my grip, moves her face towards mine.

"Not real," I remind myself. "Not real." The Loop is nothing more than a glorified video game. VE equals virtual entertainment.

Entertainment, Quantum.

The NV Visor dings again – a reminder to log in.

Dolly's image is replaced by Morning Assassin – Aiden; the many times we killed each other and how we became friends during those last few Loop days. I see his sharp features, his dark eyes. I imagine him breaking into my hotel room here in Baltimore, imagine myself springing forward to greet him with a kick to the throat using my advanced abilities. *Yes!* My finger comes up and I access my inventory list and select a bull whip, item 201, or a stick of dynamite, item 339, or my nail gun, item 31, or my Kalashnikov, item 422.

We die together, laughing our heads off. We die together.

I realize then that I can't do it, I can't log in. I know better, I remember what happened last time; I remember what it's like being stuck and the feedback...

The feedback.

I can't imagine anything more disheartening than hearing the feedback – Satan's fingernails on a chalkboard the size of Nebraska, rabid weasels with chainsaw jaws consuming your childhood home, millions of laughing bats with vampire teeth death-spiraling behind your eyes, Stalin forcing Chernobyl reactor-melt up your nose with your Nana's antique turkey baster. The NV Visor falls to my chest. Damn the feedback.

I can't do it... not yet, anyway.

About the Author

Originally from Austin, Texas, I kept Austin weird for a quarter of a century before moving to Asia. I've lived and traveled extensively through the Asian continent, staying in everything from Mongolian yurts to traditional Japanese homes on the outskirts of Kyoto. I've hitchhiked across the Punjab, met child goddesses in Nepal, visited the Tiger's Nest in Bhutan, encountered Green Tara near the Kazakhstan border, drunk soju with America's Finest in Korea -- the list goes on. Many of my 'once in a lifetime' experiences have made their way into my fiction in some way or another. Look for them.

It's safe to say I'm on a cyberpunk/LitRPG/technothriller binge at the moment. I am very interested in exploring artificial intelligence, quantum computing, virtual reality, human-android relations, addiction, mental disorders, neuronal dream worlds and advanced weaponry through my fiction.

Also by Harmon Cooper

Life is a Beautiful Thing Series (4 Books)

The Zero Patient Trilogy

Boy versus Self

Dear NSA

Tokyo Stirs

Zombie Lolita

Made in the USA
Lexington, KY
05 December 2016